Contents

CLUES TO THE EXCITEMENT ABOUT FOUR-TIME EDGAR AWARD NOMINEE

ROBERT BARNARD

"BARNARD'S WIT IS AS SHARP AS EVER. . . . THE MANY FANS OF SCOTLAND YARD'S PERRY TRETHOWAN WILL SAVOR HIS ADVENTURES IN THIS 15th ELEGANTLY SATIRIC MYSTERY."
—*Publisher's Weekly*

"PERHAPS THE MOST ENGAGING AND WITTIEST ENGLISH MYSTERY WRITER WORKING TODAY. . . . *[THE CHERRY BLOSSOM CORPSE* IS] AN INTRIGUING PUZZLE . . . AN OLD-FASHIONED WHODUNIT PEPPERED WITH COMEDY . . . ENTERTAINING READING."
—*The Nashville Tennessean*

"MYSTERY READERS WHO HAVE DISCOVERED ROBERT BARNARD WILL BE DELIGHTED WITH HIS LATEST OFFERING."—*The Richmond News Leader*

"THIS BITINGLY FUNNY MYSTERY IS ROBERT BARNARD AT HIS SATIRICAL BEST."   —*Mystery Guild Bulletin*

"THERE'S NO ONE LIKE ROBERT BARNARD IN HIS ABILITY TO COMBINE CHILLS AND CHUCKLES AND SPRINKLE THE WHOLE WITH DELICIOUS IRONY."
—*San Diego Union*

THE
CHERRY
BLOSSOM
CORPSE

Robert Barnard

A DELL BOOK

Published by
Dell Publishing
a division of
The Bantam Doubleday Dell
Publishing Group, Inc.
666 Fifth Avenue
New York, New York 10103

ISBN: 0-440-20178-0

Reprinted by arrangement with Charles Scribner's Sons

Printed in the United States of America
Published simultaneously in Canada
October 1988
10 9 8 7 6 5 4 3 2 1
KRI

THE
CHERRY
BLOSSOM
CORPSE

1

Fateful Meeting

"Oh look, darlings, cherry blossom," said Amanda Fairchild, as we sped from the docks into the centre of Bergen, and towards the bus station. She added, with a cat-like smile: "Especially for me."

I didn't tell her it was apple, and I didn't ask why it should be thought to be especially for her. I'd already had Amanda Fairchild up to *here*. My sister Cristobel, however, could always be relied upon to make the expected response.

"Why especially for you?"

"Really, darling! Do you mean to say you haven't read *Hearts in Cherry Blossom Time*? It was my Autumn title last year. It sold better than ever. If you haven't read it, darling, I assure you there's seventy-five thousand who have!"

"Seventy-five thousand! Golly!" said Cristobel.

Amanda Fairchild purred in the front seat of the taxi. I sat in the back of the taxi, with Cristobel and Jan, my wife, my son Daniel on my knee. I was glowering, and gazing bleakly ahead at the prospect of the next four days.

Amanda Fairchild had latched on to us on the boat from Newcastle to Bergen the night before. The canteen area had been very crowded, and the spare place at our table had been taken by a very drunk Norwegian, who kept pawing Jan, telling long and incomprehensible stories, and shouting "Cuckoo!" at the top of his voice. While he was at the bar getting further supplies, Amanda Fairchild commandeered his place, and repelled him vigorously on his return. At the time it had seemed as though anything would be better than a Norwegian drunk, and perhaps the warmth of my welcome to her was over-warm, to the point of being positively misleading. I don't normally pile on the warmth for over-made-up ladies of a certain age in billowing pink shantung coats, certainly not those who pat me intimately on the arm, make coy remarks about my largeness, and indulge in feeble-minded generalizations about "the male of the species" for my benefit. Nor was the progressive sinking of the heart arrested when it was revealed that Amanda Fairchild's mission in Bergen was the same as ours.

My sister Cristobel had recently fallen victim to The Curse of the Trethowans and become literary. She had converted her meagre romantic experience and her unbounded romantic longings into three novelettes that had been published by Bills and Coo, specialists in the hearts and flowers market. I suppose with a name like Cristobel there was never much chance that she would write anything other than romantic pulp. Obviously, when Cristobel told me that the World Association of Romantic Novelists (WARN for short, and I should have been) was holding its bi-annual jamboree in Bergen I should have laughed sardonically. When she said that she would love to go, but didn't have the courage to go on her own, I should have said "Tough!" and changed the subject. When she asked me directly to go with her and accompany her to the early sessions, I should gravely have assured her that I was prevented from doing so by my duties at Scotland Yard. That I did not do so may be put down to obscure feelings of guilt that I have on the subject of my sister Cristobel.

So here we all were. Cristobel, after long and tedious heart-searchings, had left her child in the care of the local vicar's wife. Jan and Daniel, my wife and son, had joined the party, Jan specifying that after one night in Bergen they would take to the mountains. I contracted with Cristobel for no less than three days of the conference before I went up to Oppheim to join them. My expectations were from the beginning of the lowest, and they assumed palpable shape in the fleshy, pink form of Amanda Fairchild.

We were hardly out of the blossom trees before the taxi drew up at the bus station. I paid the driver a sum which in England would have taken you three times round the Isle of Wight. Amanda Fairchild watched me doing it, but made no effort to contribute. Perhaps she had old-fashioned notions about not offending the pride of the male, but personally I felt that if she had 75,000 readers hanging on her every scented word, she could well be expected to chip in with the odd *krone*. The bus station, when I turned around, proved to be decidedly unattractive—not so much post-war brutalist as post-war don't care. We walked through an open foyer, and down into a dank and depressing subterranean passage.

"What a dismal place!" said Amanda Fairchild. "Creepy without being Gothic! I imagine it as the resort of drunks and druggies, and people like that."

My policeman's instinct had told me pretty much the same thing. I mentally reminded myself that the fact that a woman has a silly manner and a silly profession does not necessarily mean that she is a silly woman. We followed the directions on our conference advice sheet and went up some steps to Platform No. 7, out again into the May sunshine.

The bus that was to take us to Kvalevåg and our guest-house was not in, but another little knot of conference attenders was. Inevitably, with the British abroad, they were discussing the cost of the taxi fare.

"Darlings, was it frightfully steep?" said Amanda, swooping pinkly upon them like an Australian galah. "I had my *preux chevalier* who paid. Darlings, this is a terribly sweet man called Perry Trethowan—such a *romantic* name— from Scotland Yard, whom I positively picked up on the boat last night. Perry . . . er, *Jan*, isn't it? . . . these are all dear, dear friends of mine—" She waved her hands vaguely at the little knot, leaving me uncertain whether she actually knew any of their names, before finally she swooped unerringly on the plainest woman among them and brought her over to us.

"This is positively one of the most talented writers we have—Amarynth Dartle."

"Mary Sweeny," said the woman, putting out her hand. "I suppose if you're from Scotland Yard you'll be used to aliases."

"Not ones like Amarynth Dartle," I murmured.

"Not my idea, at all," she protested. "Dickens out of Cartland."

"Darling, your latest is without question your best," gushed Amanda. "I was riveted. I brought it as my boat reading, knowing I would be riveted, and I was. My cabin light was hardly off all night."

"You must be a remarkably slow reader, Amanda. It's only 120 pages. My publisher tells me it's gone reasonably well, but of course it's trash like all the rest."

"Mary, darling, why do you *always* disparage our calling?"

"It's not a calling, it's a trade. We're trash vendors."

"Nonsense. We are merchants of dreams."

I looked with definite interest at Miss, or Mrs., or Ms. Sweeny, thinking she might in the days ahead provide the necessary whiff of sulphuric acid in the prevailing diet of saccharine. She was a sandy-haired woman, indeterminate of feature, dressed in the cheap, sensible clothes of a woman in her forties abroad. Only a sharp, hard glint in the eye proclaimed her intelligence. She and I exchanged glances, as of one hard-boiled cynic to another.

At this moment the bus came in, and though Amanda Fairchild showed an alarming inclination to commandeer me, she was deflected by another man of the party who asked her a question about sales and contracts. The words sparked an immediate response, and Amanda launched into an authoritative disquisition which carried her on to the bus, and into a seat next to the small, thin, sandy man who had asked it. I was safe. Cristobel showed her familiar signs of panic at the thought of being left to sit with Mary Sweeny (Cristobel *clings*, you will notice), so Jan and Daniel sat with her, and I sat over the way with the trash vendor.

From farther down the bus floated Amanda Fairchild's voice, articulating the magic figure "seventy-five thousand."

"The annoying thing is," said Mary Sweeny, "that figure is probably nothing but the truth. Ten years ago if Amanda said 'forty thousand,' you could be pretty sure it was no more than thirty. Now she doesn't need to lie."

"Awesome to think of," I said. "Seventy-five thousand putting down good money for that candy-floss."

"Quite," said Mary Sweeny. "And you can afford to feel superior. I can't. The galling thing for me is that if that many put their money down for *my* candy-floss fantasies, it wouldn't be money any better spent. Amanda is supremely professional. The product is excellent. She's very good at her job."

"It's just that—"

"One wishes she could distinguish the product from *Jane Eyre*. Or even from *Precious Bane*. Though perhaps we're being unfair. Very possibly she can. Amanda has so many false fronts that she's like a magician's cabinet. I doubt whether anybody has penetrated to the real Amanda since she was thirteen. But one thing she is not, is stupid."

"That, eventually, was my impression," I agreed.

"And why," asked Mary Sweeny suddenly, "are *you* here under false pretences?"

"False pretences?" I said, astonished. "Nothing of the kind. I've never claimed to have written any of your kind of junk. I'm just here to accompany my sister."

"So I gathered from the introductions," she said, rummaging in her handbag. She pulled out at length a list of the delegates.

"I don't think I've got that," I said.

"Your sister's probably got it. She may have been keeping it from you."

"Why would she do that?"

"See here: Mrs. Cristobel Trethowan and Superintendent Trethowan. The implication is plain."

"Oh God!" I said. "Cristobel's made a boob."

"Not at all. Only husbands and wives were supposed to attend the sessions."

"Oh well—if you don't object, it can remain a

sort of official secret. After all, it may be some kind of protection."

"Protection? Do you imagine you'll need that? What kind of image do you have of us? I assure you, Amanda is not typical. Romantic novelists are very seldom romantic."

"They're very seldom novelists either."

We exchanged quick grins.

"Amanda is on the whole the exception, and even there—you notice the enthusiasm with which she responded to the words 'sales' and 'contracts'? What romantic novelists are interested in is money. You're more likely to be robbed than raped."

"Well, I think I should be able to protect myself against theft," I said.

The bus chugged along through scenery so glorious that it seemed laid out by some art-director's hand for the purpose of a Hollywood musical, in greens so rich as to be super-natural. We had no worries about where to get off, for we were to be met. We had been offered a great range of accommodations, from the international hotels run by airlines, down to camping sites—for those, presumably, whose wares had not yet found favour with the great sighing public. We had chosen one in the middle price range, some way out of Bergen. I didn't know what sort of night life romantic novelists went in for during their international beanos, but I didn't fancy being part of it. The countryside, too, seemed to offer the possibility of getting away from it all—or, to be specific, *them* all—

and I had ideas, if I were let off the leash by Cristobel, of taking advantage of it.

"I can't think what Amanda Fairchild is doing, coming to a mere guest-house," I said. "I'd have thought she would have preferred to jet-set it in one of the international hotels."

"More romantic?" suggested Mary Sweeny. "And Amanda always did like being a big fish in a small pond. Though, to be fair, Amanda these days is a big fish wherever she swims. Of the English writers she's second only to Barbara Cartland—and Barbara's not coming this year."

"Busy tending her bees, I suppose."

"Probably. And Barbara isn't getting any younger, in spite of all the evidence to the contrary. Amanda will be Queen of the British bees at this conference. As far as sheer awfulness is concerned, though, she will face very stiff competition from one or two of the Americans."

"Oh God," I breathed. "What have I let myself in for?"

And I went rather quiet for the rest of the journey.

We arrived at Kvalevåg after about forty minutes, and were indeed met at the roadside by a spare lady with a ramrod back, dressed in rather drab greys and fawns, and wearing shoes so sensible as to verge on the downright. She shook each of us by the hand, unsmiling, and to all of us murmured the formula "Good afternoon. Welcome to Kvalevåg." Then she directed a young man to pile our luggage on to a trolley, and led the way down the little dirt road towards the guest-house. We followed obediently, rather like

a scout troop, and if we let out "oohs" and
"aahs" at the scenery, it was, I assure you, scenery so indescribable in its loveliness that they
were perfectly appropriate responses. Finally
we passed a little notice saying *Kvalevåg
Gjestgiveri*, and we saw the house.

It was a square, solid, white wooden house, of
no great pretensions, but of immense charm. It
had been built, I learned later, by one of the
many Norwegian First World War profiteers, as
a summer house for his family. Less gracious
than an American colonial mansion, it looked
domestic, comfortable, welcoming. In the centre of its façade was a large porch with chairs,
above which was a little wooden balcony around
the doors of one of the bedrooms, and above this
in turn was a pair of gabled windows. But what
gave the house its real charm was its setting—
the circular path to the front door, the stunning
quiet, broken only by the birds, the trees in
which one imagined squirrels watching us, the
blossom, the spring flowers.

"*Is*n't it lovely?" said the insignificant man.

"Haven't we been clever?" said Mary
Sweeny.

The proprietress's face broke into a rare
smile. She paused to let us admire, then led the
way slowly round the drive towards the house.
We exclaimed, we examined shrubs and flowers.
Daniel ran ecstatically here and there, looking
for animals, and finding them. Even I had to
admit that, if romantic novelists had to meet
anywhere, this was undoubtedly the place. Finally we all collected on the porch, gazed at

each other, smiling at our luck, and then one by one tore ourselves from the prospect and went into the shade of the house.

Last to tear herself away from the view was Amanda. She had been unusually silent during the walk, and I had the impression that she was plotting. Now she stood there, pink, powdered, and rapt, it seemed, with the romantic loveliness of it all.

"Darlings!" she called. "We are going to have such *peace* here!"

Little, as one of her Victorian precursors might have said, did she know.

2

Dark Stranger

The sleeping arrangements for the first night were decidedly cramped. Cristobel and I both had single rooms, and a camp bed had been put up in mine for Jan's one night, and another in Cristobel's for Daniel's. However, the splendour of the surroundings made us forget any discomforts, and since we found in our room a folder with details of the conference and the participants, there was a certain grisly pleasure in going through that. Mostly this consisted of Jan laughing herself silly at the thought of what I was going to have to endure.

"Oh, look: on Wednesday there's a symposium on 'New Trends in the Romantic Hero'— Amanda Fairchild one of the panel. Do you think you might put in a contribution from the floor? And on Tuesday there's a lecture entitled 'Whither the Gothic?' What *can* that mean? Ah —here's one on 'New Markets in Eastern Europe.' You don't think they're allowed to read Amanda Fairchild in Albania, do you?"

"I shouldn't think so. I believe all pop music is banned there—it's the only good thing I've ever heard about the place—so I can't see anything so unsocially-realistic as Amanda getting through the censorship. What about the excursions?"

"Grieg's home, with a short concert of piano music. Pity you've always hated Grieg. Bus tour of Hardanger to see the trees in bloom."

"Oh God. Amanda will announce that they've come out specially for her. I'll have to make sure I'm on a different bus."

"Ah—here's a list of participants."

"I've already seen that. Cristobel has managed to imply that I'm her husband."

"Really? Is that to fend off passionate suitors? I did rather wonder whether Cristobel hoped—"

"I gather only husbands and wives are allowed to go along to the sessions. So you may still be right. Do you think she's ripe for romance again?"

"I suspect she wants a father for her fatherless child. She's been reading all this stuff about the danger of a child growing up without a male influence."

"That's nothing to the danger of a child growing up under the influence of the sort of male Cristobel is likely to saddle herself with. Better a one-parent family any day."

"Oh look: they tell you where everyone is staying. It's rather like the peerage—an order of precedence. Who's here, I wonder? Arthur Biggs—Lorinda Mason in brackets. I expect that's the sandy little man Amanda was discussing contracts with. He looks like an Arthur Biggs, though not much like a Lorinda Mason. Patti Drewe, no brackets, so presumably she writes under her own name. And Amanda Fairchild admits to no other either. But here's someone called Lorelei Zuckerman, who writes under the name of Lorelei le Neve. Now I've heard that name."

"Good God, Jan. Don't tell me you've taken to reading this sort of garbage secretly?"

"Don't be insulting. Actually, I did read one while I was at school—could well have been an Amanda Fairchild. But I decided they weren't for me. You've never found me one of the fluttering hearts mob, have you, Perry? But there's so many of them in the newsagents', you can't avoid sometimes seeing the titles and authors. How they think of the names I don't know. I expect that's where I've seen the name Lorelei le Neve."

"It's memorable," I admitted. "Only one degree less memorable than Lorelei Zuckerman."

"The funny thing is, they don't ask for them by the author's name anyway. They just ask for the latest Bills and Coo romance. I say, Perry—isn't this odd: your badge for the conference calls it the 'Romantic Novelist's Conference,' the label on your folder calls it the Romantic Novelists Conference, and the heading on all the bumf is 'Romantic Novelists' Conference.' You'd think they'd make up their minds, wouldn't you?"

"No. It proves what I've always imagined. Romantic novels are written by the semi-literate for the moronic. Amid all that breathless passion, who could give a thought to the inverted comma? Come on, let's go out for a walk in the grounds."

We collected Cristobel and went downstairs. Others seemed to have had the same idea. As we went out into the garden, Amanda was wafting back in.

"Such heaven!" she said. "Such utter, perfect heaven!"

She let the words float magically on the clear air. So, at any rate, I felt she might have put it.

Around on one of the shadowy little paths I saw the man who I thought must be Arthur Biggs, deep in a discussion of practicalities with Mary Sweeny. We took the path down to the fjord, where we found a simple little boathouse perched on a rock, and a rowing-boat. I took Daniel for a row, while Jan and Cristobel lay in the early evening sun on the wharf of the boathouse. This part of the fjord was quite narrow, because the boathouse looked towards a small island, with summer cottages dotted over it. I rowed some way, then put up the oars and lay there, parrying lazily Dan's questions about Norway with answers of unparalleled ignorance. Soon it was time to go back for dinner.

We had not been the last to arrive at Kvalevåg. When we had climbed the path and reached the garden in front of the house, we saw an immense and svelte Mercedes parked immediately in front of the porch. A uniformed driver soon trotted out and drove off. Whoever it was who had arrived, the proprietress had not been

there to meet her. She was marching back again
from the road, with another collection of people
from a bus. A jolly-looking woman wearing
sneakers, a rather voluptuous one, and a thickset
man, gaunt of face and bloodshot of eye, who
gave the impression that he had seldom been so
long between drinks. Sure enough, as the party
went up the steps of the porch towards the front
door, I heard him say in heavily accented English:

"Vair's de bar?"

The proprietress ignored him, and swept on
into the house. We lingered behind, observing
and pretending not to observe. At do's such as
this, you spend the first few hours watching the
players and deciding who there is that you could
bear spending a few hours in the company of.

"Mary Sweeny and those two jolly women
who just went past," said Jan.

"What's that?"

"You were wondering who you could manage
to put up with for the next few days."

"Smartyboots. Know-all," I said. One of the
most demoralizing things about marriage is that
it gives someone a platform ticket into your
mind. Sharing rooms in Baker Street did the
trick, too, for Holmes and Watson. "Anyway," I
said, "I expect there are others. Arthur Biggs
didn't look too bad."

"Hmmm," said Jan.

We were delaying going in, to let the new-
comers disperse, but as we went through the
porch and into the lounge we could not avoid
seeing, disappearing slowly up the stairs, a

heavy form dressed in black, taking the stairs one by one, and resting on both a stick and the arm of a companion. There floated down to us, in a thick, unlovely New York accent, words presumably addressed to the proprietress:

"I eat alone. I invariably eat alone. See that I have a table to myself. Give me *support*, Maxwell—support, for God's sake!"

Cristobel looked alarmed. Jan raised her eyebrows at me.

"*Not* destined to be one of your buddy pals at this conference, I think, Perry."

Dinner was an hour later, at seven-thirty. The normal routine of the guest-house would have seen the main meal served much earlier, but it had been changed to take in the various times of arrival of the conference-goers. When we got down to dinner there was no mistaking the important, Mercedes-borne new arrival. Seated, vast and immobile, at a table to herself was a malevolent-looking old woman, her hair dyed an aggressive black, and dressed in a shiny black material that may not have been bombazine but was what I have always imagined bombazine to look like. She was smoking a small cigar while she waited for her soup, and in front of her was a half-bottle of brandy, and a decanter of water. She poured from both into her tumbler, inhaled on her cigar, and sat there silently watching us from her malevolent little eyes.

"Nice," muttered Jan.

The single table stood out the more because the rest of us were seated at two long tables—not crowded together, but still forced to mix, to make ourselves known to each other. I think in normal circumstances this would have worked very well, and brought the party happily together. But there we were making embarrassed little social gestures under the dark, contemptuous eye of the Buddha in black over by the fireplace, sipping periodically from her brandy and water. It was also ludicrous. I began to laugh, and Jan, on the other side of the table, began to giggle too. Cristobel said "Shh," scandalized, so we both subsided. Everyone seemed subdued, even Amanda, who had come down intending to queen it, and found herself talking in hushed tones, for no pin-downable reason.

From the next table I heard a quiet-looking young woman whom I took to be the black monster's companion say in a whisper: "Lorelei Zuckerman," and then repeat it to another questioner.

"It's Lorelei Zuckerman," I hissed to Jan.

"Well, I didn't think she looked like a Doreen Smith," she hissed back.

Meanwhile the bombazined figure was taking in a deep slurp of soup, alternating this with a sip at the brandy and water, her eyes all the time on us, as if evil-mindedly contemplating our idiocies. For an instant social icing-over, her presence would have been hard to beat, so that even those of us who had bought a bottle of wine hardly felt more cheerful or more relaxed with our fellow delegates by the time the meal ended. I formed the conviction that I was going to have to make for the bar when this gastronomic experience was over. But before that could happen, there was an interesting little scene.

The meal finished with an extremely good crème caramel. The cooking at *Kvalevåg Gjestgiveri* was not adventurous but it was extremely satisfying, and as over the next few days I got to know the horrors of the cooking in the larger hotels of Bergen I came to appreciate it more and more. When the meal was over there was nothing to keep us there. Our conversational gambits were nervous and short-lived, as if we knew we were being bugged by the KGB. We began pushing back our chairs and discussing what we would do next, and we did not notice that Amanda—in a vivid green and over-dressy frock—had swanned it over from her table and had gushed her way up to the black Buddha.

"I *couldn't* forbear coming over to say hello," she cooed. The black eyes stared at her, the mouth puffed cigar smoke in her direction. "A little bird told me you're Lorelei le Neve." A pudgy hand went down to the brandy and water, and the glass was raised, while the eyes continued to regard Amanda consideringly, as if she were a rat in a laboratory. Even Amanda faltered. "And I just wanted to say . . . to say how *very* much I enjoyed *The Belle from Baltimore* . . . and *all* your other lovely stories . . ."

She faded into silence as she met with no response. Then she pulled herself together, and with a sort of bravery that I admired her for, she thrust forward her hand, and said:

"I'm Amanda Fairchild."

It was touch and go. Lorelei Zuckerman gazed speculatively at Amanda's beringed hand. Then slowly, with palpable reluctance, she raised her own pudgy mitt towards it. Flesh touched flesh, for perhaps half a second.

"Good night," said Lorelei Zuckerman.

She beckoned to the pale young girl whom I had taken to be her companion, and together they painstakingly raised the Zuckerman bulk from the table. The ridiculous thing was that none of us liked to help, or to precede her out of the dining-room. We stood there, awkwardly, as if we owed her deference, and we made a sort of path, down which Lorelei Zuckerman royally hobbled, like a larger and infinitely less genial Queen Victoria. No one, however, raised loyal hurrahs. We stood there sheepishly until we heard the sound of Lorelei and her muted companion cross the lounge and start up the stairs.

"Phew. Thank God," I said. "She's not going to the bar."

Some breaths were let out, one or two people giggled, and we made our way out of the dining-room. Some of us made for the bar, some of us went for a twilight walk around the gardens, though in fact by the time half an hour had passed almost all of us were down there in the bar.

That there *was* a bar had been attested by the gaunt man we had seen arriving. He turned out to be a Finn, and at dinner he had smelt spirituous and been virtually incoherent. This had been tested by Amanda, who had sat opposite him and had transmitted her full artillery of blandishments through the haze, with no effect. Now he led the way back there, clutching the dregs of a bottle of white wine he had drunk with his food. The bar was in the basement: an unlovely, plasticated room which contrasted sadly with the rest of the house and looked like a reluctant concession. Its stocks were bare—one brand of each drink, and that not the cheapest. I learned later that it was the only place in Kvalevåg where any sort of liquor could be obtained, and was, in the long, winter months, the resort of a few of the braver or more raffish men in that straggling rural community. There were one or two such there now, kept in stern check by the proprietress and by the young man who had brought our luggage along, who did most of the serving behind the bar. The locals regarded us with peasant curiosity, and no great approval, and before long they slipped out and left the place to us. As we stood by the counter wondering what we could afford, I felt constrained to say to Amanda Fairchild:

"That was brave."

"Darling! Positively my finest hour!" she returned, flashing me a brilliant smile. I regretted saying anything, but luckily she went and sat with someone else.

The relief of Lorelei Zuckerman's departure relaxed us all, and we managed to form up into compatible little groups, as Jan had predicted. I teamed up with Mary Sweeny and with the jolly-looking American woman, who turned out to be Patti Drewe. Cristobel also sat with us,

silent but apparently happy. Jan had slipped off
after dinner to put Daniel to bed, but she joined
us after a short while. Daniel was totally exhausted.

"Though I did have trouble at first," she said.
"He kept saying he didn't want to be up there
with that black woman. 'She's like a great big
black SLUG,' he kept shouting. God—I hope the
walls aren't thin! In the end he quietened down
when I promised to lock him in."

"He's hit the nail on the head, though," said
Mary Sweeny. "That's just about what she is."

"It's just incredible she's here," said Patti
Drewe. "I've never seen her before, never once,
not at any conference or get-together or launch-
ing-party or anything. Rumours I *had* heard. In
person, no."

"Do you have a lot of these jamborees in the
States?" I asked, in fascinated horror.

"We tend to split up, have smaller conventions. You know: the Historical, the Gothic, the
straight Romance, and so on. Lorelei writes in
pretty much all the categories, but never once
has she come. As I say, there have been whispers
about her. Now I know they're all true."

"Is she well-known?" I asked.

"Is she ever! One of our top earners, let me
tell you. She may not be quite our Barbara Cartland, but she's certainly as big with us as
Amanda Fairchild is with you."

"Such contrasting types!" said Cristobel,
plucking up courage. "Amanda being so outgo-
ing."

I realized with a sick feeling in my stomach

that Cristobel actually liked Amanda. I'd known she had lousy judgment about people since I'd learned who the father of her child was.

"Quite," said Patti Drewe crisply. "I suppose you could say they're the two ends of the spectrum. Does a spectrum have ends?"

"And what," I inquired politely, "do you write?"

"Gothics," said Patti. "With the occasional historical thrown in."

"Whither the Gothic?" I murmured.

"Oh God—don't mention that session. I've been roped in to be on that goddam panel. Hey," she said, turning to Mary Sweeny, "you write Gothics, don't you?"

"Now and then. And if you're going to ask me 'Whither the Gothic?' you can save your breath. Backwards, I imagine. It's been going backwards since Mrs. Radcliffe. I've no ideas on my trade. I'm on the committee for this damned beanfeast, and I just recruited the panels. The only perk you get for all the work is that you can keep yourself off things like that."

"I hope you recruited Lorelei Zuckerman for one."

"I wrote. When I knew she was coming I really tried. I asked her to be on 'Romance and the Changing Morality.' I got back a postcard with 'No. L.Z.' on it."

"She has *charm*," said Jan. "It oozes out of every pore. Oh, look, there's the poor little companion person."

I looked with curiosity at the companion. For once Jan seemed to have got it wrong. She was a young girl, perhaps twenty-five or so, and pretty in an unflamboyant way. She was quiet, muted, perhaps even repressed, but she didn't look downtrodden—and certainly not "poor little."

"Her name is Felicity Maxwell," whispered Patti Drewe. "Nice, I *think* . . ."

If I was looking at her with curiosity, so were the rest of the bar. I'm afraid that my congratulations to Amanda had been followed by others, and she had reverted to her usual rather overbearing form. As Felicity Maxwell stood by the bar, ordering a glass of wine from the boy-of-all-work, Amanda swivelled round in her chair and said with serpentine sweetness:

"Have you put the poor old thing to bed?"

Felicity Maxwell let a second elapse.

"Mrs. Zuckerman is very tired. She is not used to travelling." She turned round to make her remarks more general. "I'm sorry if she cast a bit of a blight tonight. She's not real companionable."

"More mildly it could not be put," muttered Amanda, so as to be heard.

"But please don't ask me to gang up on her. I owe her a lot."

And Felicity Maxwell, who must have had a penchant for hard nuts, went to sit beside the Finn.

"I'd have to owe her half the National Debt before I'd consent to be nurse-companion to Lorelei Zuckerman," whispered Jan. "She must be afraid that anything she says will get back."

And I supposed that must be it. Anyway, with that subject taboo, and us feeling ever so slightly reproved, everyone got down to talking about the conference, money, the excursions, money, current trends in the market, money and so on. I sat back and surveyed my companions for the coming week. Our table you know, and we were far and away the jolliest of the lot. Patti Drewe and Mary Sweeny turned out to be a tremendous downbeat partnership, Patti with her stories of horrendous promotional tours through the deadlands of the Midwest, Mary with her accounts of the moral, social and behavioural guidelines laid down for regular Bills and Coo authors. We all had a pretty good time. Next to us at a table to themselves (because no one else would sit with him) were Felicity Maxwell and the Finn. I'd had a nasty experience with a Finn on a previous occasion, and it clearly was not destined to be a one-offer. This one was sodden, and was telling Felicity at great length the story of his wife's infidelities, which—as far as one could penetrate the linguistic undergrowth— had ended with her running away with a piper. This, initially so romantic-seeming, became less so after Felicity by patient questioning managed to establish that he meant a plumber.

"He's *always* like this," said Patti Drewe. "He's been at the last three conferences, and he's always full to the eyebrows. Apparently drink is a twenty-four-hour occupation with him."

"But how on earth can he write?" asked Cristobel.

"If Scott Fitzgerald could write *The Great Gatsby* while half sloshed, I'm sure this one could write his sort of garbage while pissed out of his mind," I said reasonably. Cristobel looked hurt, but whether at my language or my estimate of romantic fiction I could not decide.

"You wouldn't mind," said Mary Sweeny, "if his wife had *just* left him, and he was in a state of shock. Actually, he talks about the same thing at *every* conference, and last time I established that she'd actually left him in 1970. It does rather dry up the well-springs of human sympathy."

At the next table, Arthur Biggs was holding court. That was rather what it looked like anyway. He had his wife with him, and the voluptuous American novelist ("Straight," said Patti Drewe, referring apparently to her novels rather than her sexual preferences). Biggs was— not pontificating exactly, but talking in a pretty uninterrupted flow. The two ladies were hanging on his every word, laughing obediently at his every joke, nodding periodically, or saying "Right." Even his wife was. I thought it rather unnatural.

"He likes worship," said Mary Sweeny. "Or respectful admiration, at any rate. He's written a history of the romantic novel, from *Pamela* to the present day. It's called *Happy Tears*."

"Golly!" said Cristobel, "Think of the reading involved. It must have been terrible."

I could go along with that.

And at the other table Amanda Fairchild had cornered a white Kenyan. She had made some play at dinner for the Finn, as I say, but had made no progress through his sodden self-absorption. Felicity Maxwell was much more successful with him because she was used to listening, which Amanda certainly was not. The Kenyan had arrived just before dinner: a rather large type with the air of a rugby player and a broken nose. He was coping with Amanda very capably, as if he knew the type well and had the necessary humorous tolerance to deal with it. And coming from where he did, he probably knew it very well indeed. I had read a bit about the Kenyan settler families.

"I do so admire *men* who can write for the romantic market," Amanda was cooing (quite insincerely, I suspected, for I was sure she preferred men who wrote tough fist-in-the-groin adventure stories, though these usually turn out to be small and weedy men who have regular dates with their psychiatrists). "I admire you for making the leap of sympathy involved. Such a leap it must be—for a *manly* man like yourself!"

The Kenyan shrugged.

"It's a market, like any other."

"Oh, but hardly—"

"When the things I was doing in Kenya dried up and I thought of trying writing, I looked at the market to see what sold. Romance seemed to be world wide. Certainly in Africa it's romance all the way: everyone reads them, whites and blacks. They're always about whites, but the blacks read them just the same."

"Really?" said Amanda, with a frown of concentration on her face. I fancied she was wondering whether she could dare to make one of her next romances multi-racial, and probably rejecting the idea.

"So I studied the form. Matter of fact, what I did was read Lorelei Zuckerman."

"*Did* you?" said Amanda, with more than a touch of frost in her voice.

"She may look like the Black Death, but as far as knowing the market and supplying it are concerned, she's the cat's whiskers. Have you read *Love Song at Eventide*? Bang on target in the 'straight' market. Or *Dark Peril?* Bang on target in the Gothic market. She's a one-woman market-survey, in fact."

"You feel that, do you?" said Amanda, very distantly.

"Then there's *The Belle from Baltimore*. Margaret Mitchell and water, of course, but it shows she really knows her onions in the historical field too."

"Yes. I read that. Very competent."

"I tell you, I learnt everything I know from her. She's—"

"Well," said Amanda briskly, getting up in a shower of green and little royal waves, "bed, I think. I don't know about you, everyone, but I have *masses* of things to do tomorrow. *Oceans* of people to see. *And* a signing session. This conference is really going to be *such* a whirl! So it's beddy-byes for me. *Good* night, darlings!"

The words were warm, but the exit was chilly. We all looked at each other.

"Did I say something wrong?" asked the Kenyan.

Most of us by now had subsided into cautious giggles.

"I suspect we have seen the beginnings of a great rivalry," said Arthur Biggs.

"The contest for Queen of the May has opened," said Mary Sweeny. "Or perhaps it should be Cherry Blossom Princess."

"Amanda," said Patti Drewe, "is choosing her weapons."

3

The Rival Queens

❁

The opening session of the congress was held
next morning in the Scandilux Hotel. The hotel
itself was pretty much the type of place its name
suggested, but it was situated near the harbour
and the Hanseatic houses of Bergen, so if you
could get near a window it was tolerable. The
walk there had been fine too. We had dawdled
along from the bus station, through the centre
with its cherry and apple blossom (with no
Amanda to grab credit for them), then through
the fish and flower market in the morning sunlight. On this occasion the luxurious blooms had
to contend with the powder blues, the blossom
pinks, the springtime greens of the outfits of the
various conference-goers (not to mention their
feathery or ferny hats), as they swanned their
way through, cooing their enthusiasm. Jan and
Daniel were to take the train later in the day to
Oppheim, so I said goodbye to them in the market (Daniel being very offhand, for he was rapt
over a fish in a tank of water that before long—

though we didn't tell him this—would be knocked on the head when a buyer came along). Then, with sinking heart, I accompanied Cristobel to the concrete and glass splendours of the Scandilux, and through to its mauve-hessian and brass interior.

Here, up on the fifth floor, and in the ante-room to one of its big conference chambers, one could see the assembled delegates for the first time.

"Gosh!" said Cristobel in wonder. "All those wonderful writers together in one place."

Gosh was about the word for it. A-sea on waves of pastel shades, topped by wavelets of blue rinse, green rinse and purple rinse, I had to restrain my impulse to turn full circle and march straight out through the door. Meetings of old friends and enemies were producing more "Darlings!" in more intonation patterns than a phonetician could conceive or interpret; reunions were being undergone, new alliances formed, animosities refuelled, and everyone was enthusing about something or other. The hats were of a vegetable splendour that one saw at Tory party conferences fifteen or twenty years ago, now rare in the age of the grocer's daughter. It was impossible not to feel that the male delegates cut a very poor figure of it, sartorially and in every other way, except for a tall and splendid figure in tribal robes who came from Nigeria. The rest of us felt like sparrows in a cage of galahs, and our instincts told us to lie low, or cringe.

In the thick of the "Darlings!" and the en-

thusi-moosy was Amanda. Superb in a full or-
ange coat, with yellow silk scarf and a yellow hat
with a great feather that tickled her ear provoc-
atively, she stood in the centre of the room,
clutching her welcoming fruit juice, and turning
this way and that to greet, wave, condescend to
and wave eyelashes at this or that attender at
the congress. No one, for one moment, was to be
in any doubt that she was the centrepiece of this
conference. Amanda, quite consciously I'm
sure, was forging her party, gathering supporters.

"You'd think, wouldn't you, that Amanda was
President of WARN, to watch the way she goes
on?"

Mary Sweeny, alert and cynical in the bright
morning light, had appeared at my elbow.

"And isn't she?"

"No. The President is Carolyn Fortune. What
we really need to improve our image is a com-
mon-sensical, down-to-earth president—"

"Someone like you?"

"Right, but not on your life. What we've actually got is a sort of paperback reprint of Amanda.
See—she's over there—" she pointed to an
American lady in powder blue, with pink-rinsed
hair—"and she's having to queen it to a rather
small group. Amanda's playing her version of
the Queen, so poor Carolyn's having to content
herself with being Margaret Thatcher. I
wouldn't mind betting her nose is out of joint."

"What does she write?"

"Bodice-rippers, mostly."

"What on earth—?" I began, but then I thought I knew.

"Right. Historicals with a spicing of sex and sadism. They're doing very well on the American market these days. I'm thinking of going in for them myself."

"Undeterred," I said, "by the heavy burden of research that would be involved."

"Quite. If Amanda Fairchild can send her heroine by train to Brighton in Regency England, clutching a photograph of her beloved to boot, I think the rest of us should be allowed to get away with historical murder too. Carolyn Fortune had Mary Queen of Scots and Bothwell spend their honeymoon at Balmoral."

Cristobel had drifted away, finding, I think, our cynicism distasteful. She was now by the bookstall, which was well-stocked with a selection of the works of various prominent attenders at the Congress, as well as a fat and heavy directory called *Twentieth-Century Romantic Novelists*, and Arthur Biggs's *Happy Tears*. I was just about to stroll over and resume my protective role when I saw one of the few young men in the gathering start up a conversation with her, and Cristobel look up, eager and grateful. I held back, benevolently.

It was at this point that one of the most dreadful things in a ghastly morning happened to me. Mary Sweeny had been seized on by another practitioner of her craft, and they were deep in Gothic mysteries, so I was standing there, tall and alone, a bulky lighthouse in a pastel sea, when suddenly a green-rinsed American harridan waltzed up to me, peered at my identification tag, and said:

"Perry Trethowan! I'm real pleased to make your acquaintance. I just *adored* your last!"

"I—I—" I began, apoplectic with horror, but she had sailed benevolently on to further prey, and I was left nursing the stigma. After this low-point my instinct was to withdraw from the possibility of further humiliating errors. Seeing Cristobel still eagerly conversing with the bony but pleasant-looking young man, I withdrew to an unpeopled corner of the room, and watched.

What had seemed on our first entrance to be a sea, was gradually sorting itself out into a series of ponds. Delegates, in other words, were beginning to cluster together in groups, often groups around someone. There was Amanda's group, of course, but this was beginning to disperse, and Amanda was looking round distractedly, apparently having other fish to fry. From some of the other groups was to be heard the sound of sycophantic laughter, or murmurs of enthusiastic assent. One of them was clustered around Arthur Biggs, and I wondered—

"Peregrine!" came the unwelcome voice of Amanda Fairchild. When had I given her permission to use my Christian name? How had she found out the full form of it? She was floating round vaguely in my vicinity, peering shortsightedly in search of someone. "You really *mustn't* stand there all stand-offish and Scotland Yard, you lovely man," she continued. "With so *few* men around, and even fewer *real* men or *attractive* men, you really ought to make more effort . . . *Spread* yourself around!"

She fluttered two large eyelashes in my direction.

"It's all a bit overwhelming," I muttered.

"Of course. It must be. So literary and all that. Darling, you haven't seen my Australian publisher anywhere around, have you?"

"I'm not sure that I know what an Australian publisher looks like. Do they carry koala bears with 'Write me' on them? I haven't heard an Australian accent yet, anyway."

"Oh dear, I *must* find the child. We *must* talk, and I've got an interview with the local paper in ten minutes."

She wafted away in graceful distraction, and I resumed my contemplation of the scene. The groups still intrigued me, and I began to work out in my mind the people who were being deferred to. Notables of some kind they had to be. Before long I had my solitude interrupted and my guesses confirmed by the American lady who last night had been talking to Arthur Biggs in the bar.

"Hi!" she said. "You're the Scotland Yard man —right? I wish I wrote crime, then I could have an excuse for grilling you. I'm Maryloo Parker, by the way. I can see you're standing there trying to make order of this chaos."

"That's right," I said. "I've already got my suspicions."

She was smart verging on the alluring, in browns and greens, thirtyish, with an amorous eye. I classed her with the nobody's-fool group, and thought we might easily get along.

"See that group around Arthur Biggs? Well, he's the author of *Happy Tears*, A History of the Romantic Love Story."

"I know."

"Well, he's preparing a new edition, and they're sucking up to him, hoping for a mention. The Americans are wasting their time, because he only deals with the English ones, and that's not going to change in the new edition. I know because I did my stuff on him last night. But he also has a review page in *Cosmopolitan Woman*, so they probably think it's worthwhile."

"I see. I rather thought the groups might be centred on reviewers—is that right?"

"Most of them. There's Margaret French of *Woman in the Home*. Betty Morgan of *New York Lady* and that's Everard Manning of *Boudoir*— he's a buddy-pal of Arthur Biggs, on a you-scratch-my-back basis. The other groups are mostly around publishers. Those two—" she pointed to a jolly lady and a serious one, with an enthusiastic mob of people milling around them —"they're from Bills and Coo. Hard-headed ladies, hard-headed firm, so they're wasting their time, mostly. That guy there is Marriott Dulac from Lockett Press, of Boston—our equivalent of Bills and Coo, an efficient mass-market operation. He's interested in bed—and they'd better provide it if they're young enough to be interesting and want to get on his list."

"This is all fascinating," I said. "Who's your publisher?"

"Lockett Press," she said, and she raised an eyebrow meaningfully. But before she could pursue this further she was grabbed by a friend, and I went walkabout around the room.

Amanda Fairchild had met up with her interviewer. Copies of *Bergens Tidende*, the local daily, had been scattered on a table, no doubt by the reporter, and it had a banner across the front page announcing the Congress, with pictures of the various romantic notabilities who were attending. A glance at the front page of the paper suggested it was of a dullness quite monumental, the sort of thing the Ayatollah Khomeini's followers might be permitted to read during Ramadan. But perhaps if you understood it, it was real snazzy. The emissary from the paper was closeted with Amanda in two armchairs in a bleak little niche. She looked like one of those hard-faced women who have done well out of the feminist movement. It could hardly be easy, however, to engage Amanda on an ideological plane, and I didn't fancy her chances of pushing la Fairchild into a corner.

"But darling, if we believe in women, as a sex, then surely we want them to be as *feminine* as they possibly can, don't we?"

"But surely in insisting on women's traditional roles as wives and sweethearts, you merely enforce those roles. This sort of escapist fantasy—"

"Escapist? But it's what women *want*!"

"Why is it in your books that women's happiness is always dependent on men? Women today feel—"

"Darling, why is it that feminists always say 'women feel' when what they really mean is 'feminists feel'? It's very dishonest, because it's not at all the same thing. Darling, I respect your opinions, truly I do, but I do feel that I have *rather* more right than you to say what the average woman feels, considering my readership."

"*Many women feel,*" came back the interviewer, through gritted teeth, "that women should be encouraged to find their happiness in a loving community with other women, rather than in dependence on one man."

"Well, darling, all I can say is that if you believe *that's* likely, you're displaying a tendency to escapist fantasy well beyond anything you could attribute to my readers!"

Feeling, obviously, enormously pleased with herself at this put-down, Amanda looked up, and seeing me lurking near she flashed me a conspiratorial and intimate smile. I moved hastily away. Over by the bookstall Cristobel was now on her own, but looking quietly pleased with herself.

"Found a friend, I saw," I said.

"I don't know about that," said Cristobel. "But we did have an *awfully* interesting conversation."

"You're not going to tell me he writes romantic novels? He looked quite sensible."

"Well, he does. He's an ex-monk, and he took it up when he lost his faith and had to leave the monastery."

"Good God—that's a pretty funny change of allegiance. I can't imagine he has much to bring to the hearts and flowers market."

"I think he could bring an *awful* lot of interesting perspectives," said Cristobel, setting her chin at an obstinate angle that I knew very well from childhood. "I do wish you didn't always have to be so cynical about everything, Perry."

So I held my peace until a gong sounded and we all trooped into the conference room, and took our places on hard, square red chairs. We gazed up at the members of the committee, sitting in line on the platform, of whom I knew Mary Sweeny and Arthur Biggs, and could identify the President, Carolyn Fortune. It was her big moment at last, and she washed forward to the microphone in her pastel-blue outfit, and did her third-carbon version of the Amanda Fairchild manner.

"Friends—darlings—all of you lovely people out there—I just want to start this very exciting conference by saying a very big hello, and welcoming you to this lovely, lovely city of Bergen, Norway, the home of—" a quick look at her notes—"Grieg, Ibsen, and all those marvellous Viking kings and warriors and people. I just know we're going to have a fabulous time, the kind of experience that will enrich our work, and that we shall remember for the rest of our lives." (That last bit turned out to be true for many of the delegates, anyway.) "Now, darlings, before I tell you about all the lovely things we've got lined up for you this week, I want us to be serious for just one moment. Since our last conference in Edinburgh, England—" (ouch!)—"we have lost by death two very dear members of our association. They were Mary Jane Knapp, who wrote many of those wonderful hospital romances published in the name of Evelyn Deane, and Suzanne Manners, who wrote several of the 'Lucinda-Jayne, Confederate Spy' historical romances."

"Ghost writers in the sky," I muttered to Cristobel.

"I want you to be silent for a moment, to remember their very great contribution to our art."

We were silent for Mary Jane and Suzanne, except Maryloo Parker, sitting behind me, who seemed to be snuffling delightedly at my joke.

"Now to happier things, darlings. As you'll see from your programme, we have this afternoon a very exciting lecture by Miss—er—ah—Jack—I think it's Jack-hellen, of the English Department, here in Bergen, Norway on—"

There came from the back of the hall the sound of a door opening, and then the sound of slow, heavy footsteps and an unmistakable New York voice, not hushed one whit to suit her late arrival.

"Right. Steady. I'm all right now. Go forwards."

"—on 'Pamela—Romance or Realism?' I'm sure we all appreciate—"

"No. Not there. Too far back. I shan't hear if I sit there. Not that I want to."

"—the kindness of Miss—er—Jackhellen in coming to—"

"Further. There's a seat on the aisle there. Damn these chairs. They've got arms. Can you squeeze me through?"

"—and I know you're going to give her a wonderful reception."

"Right. I'm in. You sit there, Maxwell."

The mountainous bulk of Lorelei Zuckerman, still in her shapeless but aggressive black bombazine (or whatever) garment, had been aided slowly and painfully through the hall by Felicity Maxwell, and squeezed gingerly on to one of the Hotel Scandilux's unsuitable chairs. Her thick New York drawl echoed over the chairwoman's microphoned coo whenever she had a need or a desire for Felicity to fulfil.

"And now we have a *small* change in the programme which I know is going to thrill you—"

"My handkerchief, Maxwell."

"Unfortunately, Margaret Bond has had to drop out of the symposium on Second Chance Romances on Wednesday—"

I turned to ask Cristobel what in the world Second Chance Romances were, then once again I thought I knew, so I shut up.

"—but I've been on the telephone this morning to Lorelei Zuckerman, and I'm happy and grateful to be able to report that she has consented to go on the panel in place of Margaret and give us the benefit of her experience and her truly miraculous expertise."

"On the financial aspect. I'll talk about the financial side. That's all."

Lorelei Zuckerman's speaking voice commandeered the hall. The president cooed nervously.

"Quite. That's perfectly understood. And it's not a side any of us would want to ignore, is it?"

"Sure isn't."

The business of the morning crept edgily on. A financial report was presented by Arthur Biggs in a dry, mildly pompous manner. A discussion was set in train as to where the next meeting should be held in three years' time, and there was a general preference for Paris, France, though since the romantic novel apparently does not flourish in that country of cynical amorousness, there was some doubt whether they had enough active members there to organize it. Throughout the business and discussion Lorelei Zuckerman commented, or commanded Felicity, both in her heedless and high-handed manner. It tensed me up no end, and I could see it made the speakers very jumpy. By about twelve o'clock things were beginning to wind down, and not long afterwards the President announced that:

"I've only one more thing to say, and that's the pleasant news that a lovely, lovely Norwegian cold table lunch will now be served."

She must have pushed a button somewhere, because the doors at the back now opened, and trolleys laden with food and wine began to be wheeled in and put into position on two or three long tables at the back. Everybody perked up visibly: this was the thing to give one the stiffening to face up to *"Pamela*—Romance or Realism?" in the afternoon. Everyone got up, began chattering, went to inspect the food, and soon began collecting plates and helping themselves in the approved manner to bits and pieces of this and that. Cristobel piled a plate high—she has a healthy, Girl Guide's appetite—and her morning was made by her being chatted up again by the renegade monk. I got some remarkably good prawns, and some salmon, but to prove that into each life some rain must fall I somehow found myself in a circle around Amanda Fairchild.

"*Such* a silly girl they sent to interview me. Did you hear me put her down, Peregrine? She kept going on about escapism and sugar-coated dreams and male dominance and goodness knows what. I don't know what relevance she thought it had. By the end I was *hardly* getting a word in—imagine, darlings!—so I sent her away with a flea in her ear. Then I *crept* like a little *mouse* into your interesting session. Unlike some . . ."

She looked towards where Lorelei Zuckerman was still solidly seated in the body of the hall. Felicity Maxwell had run backwards and forwards, and had procured a little table, as well as a carafe of water to go with the half-bottle of brandy she had brought with her. Now Lorelei Zuckerman sat over a substantial plate, from time to time sending Felicity running back to the table for further helpings of anything that had taken her fancy, and obviously getting great pleasure from seeing her jump up and run. Whether Felicity herself got to eat anything at all I could not see.

"*Such* a dreadful woman," said Amanda complacently. "I really can't imagine Lorelei Zuckerman *having* a second chance romance, can you?—whatever her *startling* expertise in writing them."

We all laughed—dutifully, but a little nervously. Lorelei Zuckerman had that effect on people, I noticed.

"But she certainly could be interesting on the financial side," said the Kenyan, who had expressed his admiration for Lorelei the previous evening.

And even as we laughed at her, I noticed one nervous conference delegate approach, as it were, the Zuckerman throne, and put a nervous question to her. Mrs. Zuckerman masticated relentlessly, swallowed, and then replied. A further question was put, a further reply given. Amiable she was not, but I was surprised she was replying at all. Arthur Biggs drifted over in her direction, and then Maryloo Parker, then others. When the Kenyan went up to refill his plate he did not come back to our circle, and a minute or two later I saw him around the throne. Amanda Fairchild talked on, gaily, insouciantly, but soon there were big gaps in the group around her, and she could gaze through at the circle congregating round Lorelei.

Amanda could not look ugly. Honey and charm school and facial exercises over the years had built into her face a relentlessly sweet and charming expression, and thus had she gazed from the backs of countless hardback and paper-covered editions. But eyes can less easily be made to lie, and the lights from the chandelier above reflected in Amanda's moist eyes, so that they looked like a hundred silver daggers, pointing in Lorelei Zuckerman's direction. And on Lorelei's face there played something that I could only call the ghost, or parody, of a smile.

4

Whirlwind Tour

Amanda put on her next turn the following day at breakfast, and certainly succeeded in monopolizing attention. The previous afternoon and evening had been quiet (and in the case of the lecture on *Pamela* positively somnolent, for it provided an eloquent testimony of what Norwegian students are prepared to put up with). Lorelei Zuckerman had once again eaten alone at dinner, but on the way down she had stopped in the lounge, and Felicity had fetched her a sherry from the bar. While she drank it, with her familiar, compulsive sipping technique, one or two people—notably the Kenyan, who seemed to have a confident way with fearsome females —went up and passed the time of day with her, or put to her practical questions. It would be wrong to imply that with these questioners she was gracious, for grace was not in her nature, but she did reply without rudeness, or any of the other people-repellant devices which were prominent in her armoury.

Breakfast she took in her room. So at breakfast Amanda was undisputed queen. It was a cold table, with a magnificent display of cereals, cheeses, meats and types of bread and rolls. One fetched for oneself and ate as much as one could, and the only attendant in evidence was the boy who had taken our luggage on the first day. I sat there stoking up for the next few hours. I was finding, contrary to tradition, that Romance made me hungry.

"I say," I heard Amanda's voice, floating out into the chomping silence: "do you speak English?"

She was holding up a newspaper and addressing the boy, who had just brought in reinforcements of milk and ham. He was really more than a boy—a young man. He was studying English at Bergen University, so he had a smattering.

"*Could* you come over here for a moment?"

I now saw that Amanda was flourishing a copy of that day's *Bergens Tidende*, which doubtless she had grabbed on the way down. The boy went over to her table with palpable reluctance.

"Ah—now, you see there is this article about me by . . . Ragnhild Sørby."

"*Jada,*" said the young man. "She is werry vell-known."

"Fancy!" said Amanda. "Very well-known in Bergen!"

"Werry macho-feminist," said the boy, becoming more linguistically adventurous.

"The idea appals," murmured Amanda. "But having met her, I know *exactly* what you mean. Now, what I'd like you to do is cast your eye over

the piece and translate for me all the very *nasti-*
est things she has said about me. One must know
one's enemy, so *don't* pull your punches and
fudge the translation."

The boy took the paper with fresh accretions
of reluctance, and as he cast his eye over the
article his face mantled red.

"I don't know if I find words," he said.

"I can imagine not," said Amanda grimly.
"But perhaps we find them together. Regard it
as a preparation for reading . . . Swift, or
somebody of that sort. An exercise in vituperation."

"We do not do vituperation," muttered the
boy, but gamely he made a try, and in a coopera-
tive effort he and Amanda managed to convey
to the assembled breakfast-room the gist of the
piece.

"Looking like an azalea past its prime . . . a
manner compounded of gush, condescension
and affection—"

"Affectation, darling, I would imagine."

"Affec*ta*tion . . . the candy-floss dream-fac-
tory . . . reading her books is like swimming in
warm treacle . . . the lowest common denomi-
nator of escapist literature . . . she has done
more to downgrade women's estimation of
themselves than anyone since Strindberg . . .
a Quisling and a stool-pigeon from the world of
male dominance . . ."

"Well, I think I get the *gist*," said Amanda,
apparently quite happy. "Thank you *so* much." I
expected her to tip him, but she merely dismissed him with her most brilliant smile, doubt-

less regarding it as payment enough. "Well, I must say I *do* feel flattered. The *influence* she attributes to me! Such significance as a phenomenon! I'm *so* pleased to know what she said. It will enable me to thank her in the most appropriate manner, should I come across her again!"

And she smiled a smile of luxurious anticipation.

The session that morning was short, for at eleven-thirty a fleet of buses was to come to the Hotel Scandilux to take us on our tour of Hardanger. The shortness was a blessing, for the symposium on *Whither the Gothic?* might more aptly have been called *Wither the Gothic*, for it spluttered and guttered and finally died the death as speakers were reduced to suggesting, vaguely and without conviction, computers as the possible future direction. I tried to imagine word processors taking over from Frankenstein's monster and the mad wife in the attic, and failed. I had only come along to the session because I was booked on the bus tour after it. Cristobel had sat with the ex-monk for the *Pamela* lecture the day before, and she sat with him again today. My days as cicerone were over. I sat there exercising my mind with historical mysteries: the fate of Darnley, of Amy Robsart, of Louis XVII. I didn't bother with the Princes in the Tower. I had long ago decided to dissent from the conclusions of Josephine Tey's Inspector Alan Grant.

Finally the chairwoman declared that this discussion had been fascinating, stimulating, and everything it hadn't been (as chairmen do all over the world), but that the buses were waiting, and she knew we were going to have a perfectly *fabu*lous tour, so we really must get going, mustn't we? All of us who had unrestricted use of our limbs jumped up and swarmed towards the lifts and the stairs. The others were wheeled off by relatives or attendants. We emerged from the hotel on to Bryggen, blinking at the dazzling sheen of sun on water, gazing over to the cluster of white wooden houses on the other side of the fjord. As we jostled, in the manner of these gatherings, towards the buses and what we hoped would be the best seats, I witnessed an Encounter I was pleased not to miss. Amanda, resplendent in scarlet shantung, discovered that her interviewer of the previous day was to be with us on the tour, no doubt to get material for further invectives. It was with unconcealed relish that Amanda boarded her.

"Look, darling," she called, billowing out her splendid full coat, "a *peony* past its prime today!"

The interviewer was not capable, I suspected, of being ashamed, but she sure as hell looked awkward. Amanda smiled ferociously, having conveyed the information that she had read and understood, and then passed on, prancing, to another bus.

As in supermarkets, when one makes for the shortest queue one invariably gets behind someone whose goods aren't price-marked and who laboriously pays by cheque, so I made for a bus that turned out to have an arthritic American waiting to get on, and I landed up with a seat

three-quarters of the way back. Lorelei Zuckerman, by the way, was not the arthritic American. She was not coming on this trip, and neither, consequently, was Felicity. Lorelei had
announced that she might hire a chauffeur-
driven car and do the trip later in the day—a
foolish decision, I thought, since one can see so
much less from a car, but one pretty typical of
the Zuckerman.

So there I was, on the bus with Maryloo
Parker, who at least was a friendly—a poten-
tially over-friendly—soul. I looked around to see
who else I knew. The sodden Finn was lolling
over a double seat, a half-bottle of vodka pro-
truding from his pocket. However clear the day,
and it was beautifully clear, with deep blue
skies, Hardanger would be seen by him through
a thick spirituous mist. Cristobel and her monk
were sitting still farther down than me, on the
back seats, deep in discussion, probably about
sacred and profane love. Down towards the
front were Arthur Biggs and a male friend—one
so important that Mrs. Biggs had been relegated
to the seat behind, with a sallow-looking Medi-
terranean lady with whom she was trying vainly
to make conversation.

"You see Biggs's friend," whispered Maryloo,
bending close. "His name is Everard Manning."

"Oh yes—you pointed him out to me yester-
day."

"Well, at one point in Arthur's magnum opus
—you know, *Happy Tears*—?"

"I know. Actually I've got a copy," I said, a
mite shamefacedly, but taking the paperback

out of my pocket. "I picked it up at the book-stall."

"Great. At one point, as I say, during the account of the most recent trends in the romantic novel, the pen is *seized* from the reluctant Arthur's paw by Another, who proceeds to pay tribute to the said Arthur and his contribution to the art of Romance. The seizer is Everard Manning."

"Ah—buddy-pals?"

"Thick as thieves."

I turned to the relevant passage and had a good chortle at the transparent vanity of literary gents. But the book proved compulsive, at least while surrounded by so many of the writers who were its subjects. As the bus rumbled through some not-very-interesting suburb of Bergen, I flicked around in it, and finally came across Amanda Fairchild.

"One of the undoubted new stars in the romantic firmament . . . delicate understanding of the human heart . . . exquisite sense of place . . . the very English understatement of the writing . . . her ability to convey quiet yet intense rapture . . . her willingness to work within, while at the same time enriching, the romantic tradition."

Ho-hum, I thought. He even managed to include a specimen of Amanda's beautifully understated writing:

And as they gained the top of the Cathedral tower, her petite hand somehow found its way into Hereward's brown, commanding one, and the wind brushed their hair and caressed their cheeks as they stood there in rapturous silence. And Hereward, gazing down on the streets of Exeter, and then out to the hills of Somerset, breathed into Petulia's thrilled ear: "This only has meaning for me because you are here with me to see it." And he bent down and implanted a passionate kiss on her swan-like neck.

Ho-hum indeed. I began to suspect Arthur Biggs of tongue-in-cheek. However, looking forward to the front of the bus, where he was pontificating to his tame acolyte about God-knows-what, and ignoring his wife's attempts to draw his attention to the scenery, he hardly seemed to be the sort of man to have irony in him.

The scenery now took all my attention, and all of Maryloo Parker's as well. She was a lady, I suspected, who took the very commonsense view that "what were these junketings for, if not for—?" the activity she mostly had on her mind. However, we were now approaching landscape of breathtaking splendour—a contrasting blend of mountains, fields and fruit trees, and our appreciation of this contrasting pattern of greys, greens and pinks was focused—sharpened, rather—by the narrow roads, the hairpin bends, and above all the backings on to lay-bys perched over abysses. The bus driver did it as if it was all in a day's work, as no doubt it was, and he stolidly ignored the oohs and aahs and little screams of fear that came from the body of the bus. But I did have some sympathy with the girlish screamers. This looked like an area that was death to tourists: one lapse of attention, caused by the intense natural splendour, and one was over a precipice and well and truly part of that splendour. Even in a bus one's attention could only be on one's immediate situation and one's immediate surroundings. Maryloo sat there rapt.

"My Gahd, what I could make of this!" she breathed. Then she thought: "Me and two hundred other delegates."

We stopped for lunch at a little hotel perched on the hillside overlooking Hardangerfjord. It was a modern construction, dull and anonymous, and quite lacking the appeal of *Kvalevåg Gjestgiveri*. It had a large, plain lunch-room, however, and here we were fed boiled cod, boiled potatoes and boiled tinned peas. The peas, in all fairness, could hardly have been done any other way, but what they did to the cod was all the more bitter because it had probably been fished straight out of the fjord, before having all its taste boiled out with the water.

The buses had all arrived at the hotel together, and after standing for a few minutes admiring the stunning clear blue sky and the sloping orchards of blossoming trees stretching from mountain foot to the edge of the fjord we all trooped in to our dispiriting meal. I managed to get next to Mary Sweeny, which at least gave me the prospect of an agreeably vinegarish session. But I wished we could have got closer to another, fascinating combination, for about five places from us, facing each other and obviously raring to go, were Amanda and her interviewer of the day before, Ragnhild Sørby.

The Norwegian had been sat in her place before we arrived. No doubt she had *done* Hardanger in blossom time often enough before, or perhaps she was a glutton for boiled cod. Anyway, there she was sitting waiting when over billowed Amanda and insisted on sitting directly opposite. About as welcome as a breeze from Chernobyl, she ignored the scowls and the scufflings and apparently launched straight into a detailed discussion of the Sørby woman's article. Clearly it was a discussion that pulled no punches, and I wished I could have heard more of it.

Amanda had a small, slightly mousy figure in tow, who sat beside her and acted as a lay figure in the dialogue, rather as Arthur Biggs tended to use the people around him as lay figures. She was young, obviously dependent on Amanda, and she nodded periodically. Mary Sweeny whispered to me that she thought this was Amanda's Australian editor.

But if only I had been nearer the clash of battle! As it was, I only heard snatches, as the conversation died down for a few moments among the people between us.

"But darling!" I heard, as we waited for the boiled cod, "if a woman is to find her happiness with other women, why does that mean she should dress like a *frump*?" She cast a kind look at Frøken Sørby. "I don't quite see why *frump*ishness should attract other women, any more than it does men."

Ragnhild Sørby, dressed in jeans and a chunky
pullover that looked as if it had been knitted
with shredded tree bark, leaned back and then
lunged forward to reply vituperatively, but
high, embarrassed conversation breaking out
around her prevented me from hearing.

"How *old* would you say Amanda is?" whispered Mary Sweeny over the table.

"Oh golly, I don't know. A well-preserved
fifty?"

"Add five, I'd have thought."

"Wait a minute, I think there's a biographical
index at the back of *Happy Tears* . . . Yes,
there is." I riffled through the pages and found
the place. "Fairchild, Amanda—and then in
brackets Maureen Jane Shottery. Perfectly good
name, but not euphonious enough, I suppose.
Let's see: 'Amanda Fairchild was born and
brought up in Tiverton—' *no date.* I'm not surprised. Amanda wouldn't think it womanly to
tell anyone the date, nor indeed gentlemanly to
ask. Let's see: 'Went to the Guildhall School of
Music and Drama, and had a ten-year career on
stage, including Helena in *Look Back in Anger*
at Greenwich in 1960, Goneril with the Lincoln
Rep in 1966 and Shakespeare tours for the British Council. Since taking up writing romance in
1967 she has brought out over fifty books, and
now writes two a year.' Hmmm. No indication
there of age. She could be anything from twenty
to thirty-five to play Helena. The stage career
seems to have rather lacked distinction, don't
you think? Still, she really has churned out the
books."

At that moment there was a momentary lull in the conversation around us, and I caught more of Amanda's lengthy put-down.

"Women's commitment to *peace*, darling? But what *nonsense*! Women have always had the greatest enthusiasm for *war*, especially as we've never actually had to fight in them ourselves. Look at all the woman prime ministers we've had in the world recently—terrible war-mongers! Appalling battle-axes! Look at the women in the First World War who used to go around distributing white feathers to men not in uniform. The trouble with you, my dear, is that you build an absolute *sky*scraper of belief on a foundation of *myth*! Pure myth!"

As the battle was drowned again, I whispered to Mary Sweeny:

"Really she's doing quite well. That's why she made the boy go over the thing this morning: actress's instinct to get well rehearsed! I rather wish I'd pitted her against my wife on that subject."

I was frustrated at not being able to hear more of this welter-weight contest, especially as the most interesting conversation I *could* overhear was Arthur Biggs pontificating to his friend, his wife, and assorted acolytes. He was going on and on about the literary scene, about Spender and Holroyd and Brophy and Drabble, and someone called Wilson, though whether this was Angus or A. N. or even Edmund I never found out. He then went on to give a disquisition on the feminist Gothic, which apparently was the wave of the future in the romance field. I could only imagine it meant mad husbands in the attic. His style of discourse had an undertow of sneer, which somehow included not only his subject but his audience as well. He was the sort of man who, when he lent you a book, would say: "I thought it was pretty awful, but you may enjoy it." It was disgusting to see his puny shafts received with nods and smiles by his audience, and quite nauseating to note that his wife was the most enthusiastic nodder and smiler.

When we saw dishes of tinned pears being handed round, Mary Sweeny and I got up and spent the rest of the lunch-break walking around the hotel, talking about Amanda and photographing cherry blossom. When we got back on the bus most people—especially Amanda, I noticed, who felt she had won a famous victory and didn't mind telling people so —were in high good humour, and on the way back to Bergen Maryloo Parker was able to combine admiration for the scenery with sexual advances of an engagingly frank nature. I confess I was torn between a feeling of how despicable such an interlude would be, granted that I was only going to be separated from Jan for a couple of days, and another feeling that what she was offering was uncomplicated, would have no repercussions, and might be very pleasant indeed.

I had not resolved this split by the time we arrived back at Kvalevåg. And in the event my night was to be filled with another activity, equally familiar, but very different.

5

Dark Consequences

When, at about half past five, we arrived back at the *Kvalevåg Gjestgiveri*, the Romantic party had been increased by two. Cristobel had invited her monk to dinner, and Arthur Biggs had done the same for his toady Everard Manning. Cristobel asked the proprietress very timidly if that was all right. Arthur Biggs announced it, and ordered a separate table. I got the impression that he was rather miffed by Lorelei Zuckerman's solitary splendour, and wanted to assert his right to a similar distinction.

I had by now been introduced to Cristobel's monk. He was called Bernard Palterton, and he was slim, sandy-haired, and pleasant in a diffident kind of way. We did not discuss either of his vocations, religious or romantic, but he did tell me that he had published three books, and had three more completed, so he seemed to be something of a natural at the trade, in a sausage-machine kind of way. You notice I was already, in my slightly Victorian fashion, sizing up young

Bernard's potential as a provider for my sister. Well, it was high time she got married. *More* than high time, a real Victorian would have thought.

At dinner we were all quite jolly at the main table. I gave an account of my part in the pursuit and arrest of the Balham Knife Murderer, and they all showed commendably strong stomachs as they ferreted out the gory details. Crime writers, I suspected, would have been much more squeamish, but this lot wanted it all, down to the last inch of intestine. Amanda, it is true, did contribute the information that the poor man had been jilted by his fiancée at an early age, but I countered that since his childhood hobby had been cutting up kittens, the jilting should probably be seen as a result rather than a cause of his revolting activities. We ate on with relish.

Maryloo Parker was separated from me by nine or ten places at table, so she was unable to train on me her experienced artillery. Thus far I was saved from a decision.

Lorelei Zuckerman sat, as always, alone, in a hideous deep purple dress that did nothing for her. I rather thought she acted on the principle that there was nothing that would do anything for her, and flaunted the fact. Certainly one could say she made an effect. The meal that night was an excellent pork chop, followed by a baked sponge. Sip, sip, chomp, chomp she went through it, though with no other obvious signs of enjoyment. Felicity Maxwell went over from our table to offer to cut up the chops for her. Lorelei considered for a couple of seconds, uttered a simple "No," and Felicity retired, dismissed but not apparently offended.

Things were slightly merrier at the other separate table, but not much. Arthur Biggs had put on his literary historian's hat, and was giving a mini-lecture on the works of Ouida and Marie Corelli. It was listened to by his wife and Everard Manning in respectful silence, except for the fawning gestures of response—a nod, an appreciative smile, a deprecating shake of the head. Never had I seen anybody with a more rigorously trained appreciation society. The lecture passed on to Elinor Glyn, and still the nods and smiles came on cue. Chomp, chomp, slurp, slurp, nod, nod.

Dinner finished around twenty past seven. Lorelei Zuckerman was the first to leave. She took a perfectly audible last sip of her brandy and water, and shouted to Felicity. The latter had finished eating some time before, and had sat awaiting the call. She pushed back her chair and went over to hoist la Zuckerman out of hers. She was gentle but very capable physically, and she soon had her on her feet. As they were progressing out, I saw the Kenyan raise his eyebrows at Felicity and point to the exit. She shook her head, and mouthed "Half an hour." I tactfully pretended not to have heard this, but a minute or two later I heard the man explaining to his neighbour that he had been invited to have a drink in Lorelei's room, and was intending to get from her gen on how to break into the American market. I admired his courage. Talk about "into the valley of death"!

Lorelei's going, as usual, gave the signal for a general break-up. Logically it ought to have signalled the beginning of festivities, but somehow or other she seemed to constitute some dreadful centrepiece, and we rather collapsed without her. First Arthur Biggs and his party evaporated off towards the grounds, then the rest of us began scraping our chairs backwards, and making general getting-up motions.

Amanda, of course, could not simply evaporate. She had not asked her Australian editor back to dinner, and had been sitting quite thoughtful throughout the meal. Now she made motioning signs to the boy-of-all-work, who had been bringing wine to the few who could afford to drink it.

"I'm *sorry* to trouble you, but you were *so* helpful this morning, and I wondered if you *could* be an angel and translate for me a *tiny* letter I've written to your local paper. One sentence, literally *one*, I promise you."

"It is not necessary. They print in English," said the boy.

"But I want to reach the *widest* possible audience," said Amanda. "After all, *her* piece did, it will take *three* minutes—two!—no more."

The boy looked round at the proprietress, and with pursed lips she nodded acquiescence.

"Come to my room!" cooed Amanda, and sailed ahead so that she did not see the look of sheer horror that came over his face. Clearly he was convinced that he was going to be raped by this pink predator, and I must say the rest of us rather wondered too. Bravely he squared his shoulders and followed her.

So we all went our various ways. I wandered out into the grounds with Cristobel and Bernard. After we had strolled in the brilliant evening sun-and-shadow for ten minutes or so, I realized they would much prefer to be alone. Perceptive of you, Perry! Bernard was to take the last bus back to Bergen, but there was an hour or so for them to make good use of before then. I walked back towards the house, irresolute. Prudence suggested that I should shut myself in my room with a good book. I had brought with me the memoirs of a former head of Metropolitan Police, to see how many direct lies I could catch him out in. Still, it was not riveting stuff.

*Im*prudence and inclination suggested the bar. And in the bar, doubtless was Maryloo Parker . . . While I was still dithering, down the stairs came Amanda, with the waiting boy following behind with a relieved expression on his face.

"Thank you *so* much," fluted Amanda. "I *think* that puts her in her place, don't you? And you'll put it in the post-box for me? Wait . . ."

She fumbled in her bag, and I expected her to produce a fifty-kroner note, or even a hundred, to tip him. In the event it was ten. His manner of acceptance was no worse than graceless, which it probably would have been whatever the denomination of note. I had the impression that most Norwegians wouldn't recognize a Grace if it came down and landed on their head. The boy tootled downstairs towards the bar, and—quite without thinking on my part—Amanda and I slowly drifted in the same direction.

"I think just a tiny gin and tonic to take up to my room," announced Amanda. "I have an immense amount to do."

"Are you writing?" I asked.

"But of *course*, darling! I don't regard this as a holiday. I have to do ten pages of *The Pretender's Sweetheart*."

"Ah—a historical," I said wisely. "Do you have to do an immense amount of research for them?"

She shot me a sharp, intelligent glance.

"Someone has been talking," she said.

"Oh, you know what people are. Someone said you'd sent your heroine down to Regency Brighton on a train."

"Darling, I *never* discuss my books! What is written is written! . . . *Could* I have one of your *lovely* gin and tonics, do you think?"

We were at the bar, where the proprietress presided. Amanda turned from that lady's slightly grim demeanour back to me, and fixed me with her most dazzling smile. "Or should that be gins and tonic? Grammar was never my strongest point either."

But I was busy scanning the assembly. This evening there was no sprinkling of locals to gaze at us unashamedly out of cunning, peasanty eyes. Instead there was a family of four Americans, doing Norway, and there was a party of three Bavarian men, all looking like Franz Josef Strauss. One of them banged on the table for service, but the proprietress rightly ignored him.

And then there were the Romantics. Arthur Biggs with his two fans were at one table, well away from the rest. I was getting the impression that Biggs regarded himself as a Person of Consequence, who could not be expected to fraternize lightly. Then, dotted untidily round two tables, there were Mary Sweeny, the Kenyan, the Finn, Patti Drewe and—inevitably—Maryloo Parker. I had been spotted as I came in, and Maryloo was regarding me with Your Destiny written in her eyes. I wandered over in her direction, telling myself that my Destiny was still firmly in my hands rather than hers. The night, after all, was still young.

The talk, oddly enough, was drifting towards politics. Mary Sweeny started it off by saying that you could say what you liked about Mrs. Thatcher—and she could quite happily say plenty—but one thing her government had done was bring in Public Lending Rights, which had transformed the economic position of writers.

"Mind you," she said, "it would have transformed mine a damn sight more if public libraries bought as many Romances as they ought to."

The Americans were naturally avid to hear more about anything that improved the financial situation of writers, and from Thatcher we drifted on to Reagan. Patti Drewe said you could say what you liked about *him*, but he was a great communicator.

"But what exactly *is* it he communicates?" asked Mary Sweeny.

Then it was on to the next Prime Minister, the next President, and then back in history to that dreariest of topics, the Kennedy family. Maryloo Parker, who claimed to go weak at the knees at the sight of Gary Hart, had apparently been part of every abortive Kennedy campaign of the last twenty years.

"You seem to have been a willing helper," I said.

"Boy, if you were not willing, you weren't a helper," she said, making meaningful eyes at me.

From there we would probably have gone on to Kenya and South Africa, but the Kenyan, whose name I now found was Wes Mackay, looked at his watch.

"Looks like the half-hour is up," he said. "It's us for the lion's den—and I never even took a thorn out of her paw in the distant past!"

"Us?" I said, surprised, for he was jerking the comatose Finn to his feet.

"Yes—Martti and me. We were having a sherry with her last night in the lounge before dinner, and la Zuckerman asked us both up for tonight. We've been having a few chats about markets and agents and trends, and she said we could have a good confab about them. I want to get as much gen as I can about the American market. I think I showed my surprise at the invite, because she just muttered 'Too few men' as she hobbled off. I'm not too sure that Martti knows what he's in for yet."

But he managed to get him to his feet, and he steered him solicitously through the tables in the little bar, and then gradually up the stairs.

"Boy, do they have guts!" said Maryloo Parker.

"What the Finn has is alcohol," I pointed out.

"And she has been rather less fearsome, this last day or two," said Patti Drewe. "Compared to that first horrendous evening."

"Always to men—have you noticed that?" put in Maryloo. "Of course, we're all like that, but I'm a bit surprised at her. She hasn't made any nice noises in the direction of any of the women here."

"Felicity seems devoted to her—or something," I chipped in.

"But apart from Felicity, la Zuckerman seems happiest—silly word!—with men. God knows what she hopes to get out of them." She gave me her look again. "The mind boggles."

"What *is* her background?" I asked.

Patti Drewe seemed to have heard most.

"All sorts of stories seem to go around. Maybe people make them up because nothing is actually known. The one about her having been a fairground wrestler I doubt. The ones that seem to surface most often are a stint in the armed forces, the CIA, a spell in Britain, and a small-time opera singer."

"The spell in Britain didn't rub off on her accent," said Mary Sweeny.

"That sort of accent is unalterable. It's there for life, like freckles or a club foot. We're used to it in the States—I suppose it grates on you?"

"It certainly doesn't fall gratefully on the ear," I admitted, "though somehow it seems to fit the whole personality so perfectly I'm not sure I'd want her to speak any other way. I presume the lady has never been married?"

"We don't call women ladies any more in the States," said Maryloo.

"It was a courtesy title only," I murmured.

"No husband or ex-husband has ever been spotted, but it is rumoured there's been one. One *can* imagine her grinding some poor devil down to a powder, then flushing him down the john, don't you think?" She gave me that look again. "A man has many uses, and for her one would guess the principal one would be as victim."

Well, we thrashed over the subject, and went on to this and that, or rather to him or her. We did over Arthur Biggs pretty thoroughly, in hushed voices, and the Americans went to town on the conference's president. Maryloo, from time to time, trained her artillery on me, and after a bit I began to respond. Part of me still resisted, though. At five past nine I looked at my watch.

"I promised to ring Jan at Oppheim. She should have got Daniel to bed by now."

It wasn't true. I'm not sure whether it was a way of stiffening my virtuous resolve, or making sure she was there. Anyway, I slipped out, but not before Maryloo had smiled at me again with her Your Destiny smile.

The phone was in a little nook off from the main lounge. I had no sooner got through to the hotel, and they were hunting through their book for Jan's room number, than I saw Amanda swanning it down the stairs. Presumably she was taking time off from romps in the heather in '45. She was in a purply-pink dress, without coat or handbag, and altogether *au naturel*. She wafted out through the front door, and on to the little lawn in the centre of the drive. It was twilight, but still warm, and she let the wind ruffle her hair caressingly. It would have made a lovely cover.

"Jan?" I turned away from the little window that gave me a view to the front of the house. "I thought I'd ring you and tell you I will be coming tomorrow."

"I know that. I didn't think there would be anything at the conference to detain you."

"Or any*one*," I said, rather too forcefully.

"Well, I didn't think so, but—"

"How's Daniel?"

"Oh fine. He just loves it here. I think we had somehow given him the impression he'd be able to ski, but otherwise—"

As Jan talked I turned back to the window. Amanda had stepped daintily across the lawn, and was now heading towards the little tree-lined path that led down to the boathouse. The gentle breeze was still ruffling her hair, for all the world as if she were standing on a Hollywood set in front of a wind machine.

"And the hotel?"

"Perfectly all right. Not so charming as Kvalevåg, not by a long chalk, but the *scenery* . . ."

We chatted for some time, and I kept it going with question and answer, because I thought Jan's sensitive antennae had picked something up. Finally I told her that I'd catch the same train she and Daniel had taken the next day (though alas, as Amanda might have said, it was not to be), and we said goodbye. When I put the phone down it was twenty past nine, but there was still light outside. I was surprised to see Cristobel and Bernard wandering back to the house from the path that led to the road. It did not escape my supernaturally sharp policeman's eye that they were hand in hand. I went out on to the porch.

"Thought you were catching the last bus back to Bergen," I said to Bernard, trying not to make it sound too heavy-father.

"There's been an accident somewhere between here and Bergen, and it's blocked the road," said Cristobel defensively. "We've been standing up there for ages with the boy, who's meeting hotel guests. In the end someone who'd had to turn back stopped and told us. The boy says he'll let us know when the bus goes by to Kvalevåg, then we can go down and Bernard can catch it on the way back to Bergen."

"Oh, fine. I'm off down to the bar. Coming?"

"Oh no. No, I don't think so," said Cristobel, looking at Bernard.

"No, we'll just—walk around," said Bernard—not exactly soppy, but not entirely sensible either.

"Right, well, er, good night," I said, watching them go off hand in hand. I didn't go back to the bar at once. I needed to think. I went up to my room and had a cigarette. I thought. I suppose you could say I struggled with my conscience. To no avail. I stubbed out my cigarette, and went back to the bar.

But downstairs was beginning to break up. That tended to happen in Norway, the price of drinks being what it was. You buy one, toy with it playfully for as long as possible, then decide on an early night. In fact, things were a lot more fluid down there, and it was a fluidity that I cursed later, for I had no clear idea who was where for the next half-hour. The Biggs party and my party were both standing up and beginning to mingle. The lady in the family of American tourists had come over to beg autographs first from Patti Drewe, then from Maryloo Parker, and both were being gracious and friendly. Mrs. Biggs, as a relief from all that husband-worship, was talking to Mary Sweeny about the Norwegian folk-products in the local Husfliden shop. And to make my perceptions of what was going on still more unclear, Arthur Biggs sealed his growing unpopularity with me by coming up and saying:

"I say, I had no idea you were one of the Tre*thow*an family. My friend here has just been telling me—"

It is an accusation I always have great difficulty in coping with. To remain polite in such circumstances has, over the years, required an effort that has become positively physical. I tried to make polite chat about my Uncle Lawrence and my Aunt Sybilla, and then this frightful squirt Everard Manning came over too, and actually asked me questions about my father and his death. I felt I could with double justification, as policeman and as son, stonewall on that subject, and when he persisted I brusquely turned and began talking to Mrs. Biggs and Mary about handknitted sweaters. Anything would have been a relief. Then I talked to Patti Drewe, then I had a gay little sparring match with Maryloo which I won't go into, and we gradually made our way towards the stairs and up them, and then lingered in the open lounge by the main door. In the gathering gloom I saw Cristobel and Bernard making their way, hand in hand, down the path to the boathouse. Alone for a moment I found Maryloo at my elbow.

"Eleven-thirty, my room," she whispered.

But, as you no doubt have anticipated, It Was Not To Be. Maryloo was just starting up the stairs, Arthur Biggs was heading for the telephone to get a taxi for his friend, the rest of us were saying our good nights, when the whole tableau was frozen by a terrible sound.

My sister Cristobel is used to finding bodies, and she knows exactly what to do. She goes off into a spectacular fit of hysterics.

6

The Men in Blue

Amanda's body, when Bernard and Cristobel found it, was face down in the fjord, one foot still on the landing-stage of the boathouse. The billowing pink dress meant that it was bobbing up and down in the water that lapped against the pillars of the boathouse. On top of the corpse had been cast a bough of cherry blossom.

By the time I saw it, it was looking rather different. I spent a minute or two trying to still Cristobel's yodelling shrieks, which were disturbing the squirrels and the waterfowl, but then I handed her over to Mary Sweeny and ran down the path to the water's edge. It was now almost completely night, but there was a lamp on the side of the boathouse, for the benefit of night fishermen, and there was a near-full moon which made parts of the sea look like vanilla cream. Bernard had got Amanda out of the water on to the landing-stage, and was attempting to give her mouth-to-mouth resuscitation. It was the most unromantic form of oscular contact, and I could see it was hopeless. So many remarkable instances of survival after drowning seem to have taken place recently, however, that I felt duty-bound to assist the operation.

"Go up to Cristobel," I said, pushing Bernard aside. "She responds to common sense. And have someone ring the police."

I went on with the process for three or four minutes, but there was no sign of life whatsoever. I let Amanda flop back on to the wooden slats and darted up the path again. By now Bernard and Mary had succeeded in calming Cristobel, but her cow-calls had inevitably roused the entire guest-house, even to the American family and the party of Bavarians. One of these last tried to barge past me down the path, but I shoved the palm of my hand against his chest, feeling rather heroic.

"Tod," I said. *"Ein Frau ermordet."* Then, having exhausted my stock of something-like-German, I pointed to the ground. "You. Stop here. Stop them." I gestured to the assembled guests, registering that all except Lorelei were there, even unto Felicity Maxwell, looking on from the balcony in the centre of the house, and the Finn, lolling against one of the pillars of the porch. The German seemed to understand, and be pleased to be given a position of responsibility and power. "Very well. I understand perfectly," he said, in excellent English.

I walked down again along the slightly eerie dark path. I went carefully, but I knew that there could not be footprints. May was Bergen's only dry month as a rule, and the proprietress

had told us that it had not rained for ten days
before our arrival. It seemed to worry her.
Other traces of the murderer there might be,
though, and I wanted nothing disturbed. For I
was quite sure this was murder. How could
Amanda simply have fallen in, and not been
able to save herself? Anybody could simply have
clutched on to the landing-stage—unless, of
course, they had been forcibly prevented from
doing so. I looked down at the soggy branch of
cherry blossom, which after Bernard's efforts
was lying beside the body. I looked around to
make sure, and confirmed what I already knew:
there were no cherry trees on the path down to
the boathouse, or in its vicinity. The branch,
therefore, must have been fetched there, placed
deliberately there. My mind played around with
the ambiguity of the clue.

But it was useless to speculate yet. The lamp
on the corner of the boathouse cast a good light
forward to the fjord and a dim sufficiency of
light for a few yards behind the little wooden
structure. I went into the undergrowth behind,
taking the usual policeman's care. The Norwegians, I had already learned during my trip
around Hardanger, are very careful with their
countryside, treating it with all the finicky pro-
tectiveness of a house-proud housewife (and
what right have we to sneer, on second thoughts
—we, the casual chuckers-away of soft-drink
cans, crisp packets, cigarette ends, beer bottles
and broken toys, who treat our countryside as
the garbage-tips of our tenth-rate technological
civilization?). Anyway, this meant that, since

most of the trade at *Kvalevåg Gjestgiveri* in the pre-summer season had been Norwegian, there was little of the usual detritus lying around. There was a plastic wallet such as travel firms enclose tickets in, there was an empty bottle, its strong smell of spirits contrasting oddly with the natural evening smells around, there was a local bus-timetable and a copy of one of the hand-outs from the *Pamela* lecture—an incomprehensible collection of diagrams with headings like "Surface Pattern" and "Deep Structure." It was a meagre haul. I went back again to the body.

Amanda, as I had noted earlier, had gone down to the boathouse *au naturel*. The body, as it lay on the latticed wood, soaked through with fjord water, showed signs of nothing more than the billowing pink dress with, underneath, the outlines of undergarments that I mentally characterized as "traditional." Rather the sort of thing that I imagined ladies of easy virtue used if they were entertaining elderly tired businessmen. Now I noticed that, if the undergrowth around the landing-stage was nearly clear of rubbish, the water was not. I squatted on the edge of the stage, beside the one rowing-boat moored there, and picked out of the fjord a plastic container that may have held fuel for a motor boat, one of those horrible little plastic tubes that hold soft-drinks for children, some chocolate wrappings, and three pieces of paper. I retrieved everything, and was particularly careful about the pieces of paper. I took them into the boathouse, and laid them on the bench. One of the pieces seemed considerably less sodden than the others, and I was just wondering whether I could risk flattening it out when I heard noises from above: first the squeal of car tyres on gravel, then the sound of voices. I knew that sort of sound well. It said that the police had arrived.

Somehow it felt funny to be on the wrong end, as it were, of arriving police. I left the pieces of paper where they were, and toiled up the path again.

There were two police cars pulled up outside the front porch of the *Gjestgiveri*, and about five policemen cluttering up the lawn in a rather aimless manner. Their boss, however, seemed to be a mild-looking, fair-haired man, of a slim, delicate build and inoffensive manner, who was talking to the proprietress of the guest-house and the Bavarian I had left as human barrier at the top of the path. As I approached, the proprietress gestured in my direction, and I saw the policeman's pale blue eyes turn and his sandy eyebrows raise themselves.

"Ah! Scotteland Eeyard!"

The Bavarian stared at me with a new interest.

"Ach! Schottland Yard!"

It was good to know that there were some British institutions apart from the monarchy and the pop groups that still commanded international respect. I shall not try to reproduce the policemen's English, however, which can get tiresome. I was told that Norwegians do a great deal of grammar and phonetics in school, and I can only say this does them remarkably little good.

"Yes. Scotland Yard," I said, feeling like some character in a Gilbert and Sullivan opera. I added firmly: "On holiday."

"Ah . . ." The policeman looked around at the dark shapes of the assembled gawpers, illuminated eerily by the lights from the house. They had got together in a huddle now, as if to present a united front. "These are the romantic writers?"

"Mostly, yes."

"You, in your spare time? . . ."

"No," I said firmly. "My sister." I drew attention to where Cristobel was sitting under a tree regarding him with a look of romantic defiance which had no basis in common sense. Bernard, beside her, seemed to be uttering reassuring words. "That is my sister and her . . . the gentleman who was with her when they found the body."

"Ah . . . We go down?"

And so we plunged down the Stygian path, the policeman taking one of his men with him. On the way down he introduced himself as Førstebetjent Bjørhovde and his second-in-command as Sergeant Jernsletten (I only learnt much later how to spell these names, and never learnt to pronounce them). I asked if they didn't have Christian names, and he said they were Stein and Svein. That seemed much easier, so we were forced into informality by linguistic considerations. Stein and Svein didn't seem to find Trethowan very easy either.

Stein, the inspector or førstebetjent, stopped before he got to the landing-stage, and surveyed the body laid out in the powerful light from the boathouse lamp.

"It was in the water when it was found," I said. "With just a foot on the landing-stage." He nodded.

"Who is she?"

"Her name is Amanda Fairchild. Well, no it's —I forget—Maureen Something-or-other. But she writes under the name, is *known* by, the name Amanda Fairchild. Romantic novels, of course."

"Love stories for women," agreed the inspector.

"I certainly haven't heard of many men who read them," I said, stepping gingerly through the feminist minefield.

"Successful?"

"Very. One of the best-known in Britain, I'm told. Appears on television. Something of a personality."

Stein pondered for a bit.

"Jealousy?"

I shrugged.

"Maybe. Certainly I imagine she earned a good deal more than most of the writers here. But why wait and do it at the conference, when it could be done much more easily back in Britain?"

"Perhaps it—what do you say?—*got* to someone, really hurt them, when they were all here together."

"Maybe." My tone betrayed my scepticism. "I

scouted round in the undergrowth behind the boathouse here. There wasn't much that I could see, but perhaps your men may find more. I retrieved some bits of paper from the water. Probably nothing, but I thought they might float off if I didn't get them."

I gestured towards the boathouse, and he looked inside with his fair face impassive as usual. He nodded.

"Let them be. The laboratory chaps had better have them first." He thought for a bit. "You say she was very successful. And very rich? Did she wear jewels? Did she carry a lot of money with her? Where is her handbag?"

"As to jewels, she wasn't wearing any that I could see when she came down here. I was in the guest-house, you see, phoning, and I saw her go through the lounge and out to the lawn. There was certainly no *obvious* jewellery on her —there could have been a ring, maybe. Come to think of it, she never wore much jewellery, which you might have expected her to do. And she wasn't carrying a handbag when she left the guest-house."

"Did she usually carry a lot of money? There are other places to carry money, not just handbags."

"Surely. Well, I wouldn't know. If so, she certainly didn't dispense it around very readily."

"Dispense?"

"Shell out. Sorry—give it away. She was decidedly near . . . careful, in the matter of tipping, or paying her share. If you're thinking of robbery—"

"I was. Not very seriously, perhaps."

"—then she certainly didn't *look* as if she had money or valuables on her. That rules out any casual thief, I would have thought. It would have to be someone who *knew* she had something on her worth stealing. Therefore, presumably, someone who *knew* her to some degree."

Stein Bjørhovde nodded.

"And we must remember that the road from Bergen has been blocked," he said.

"So I gather. For how long?"

"Since about a quarter to eight. A terrible accident—the sort we get when the tourist drivers start arriving. Here in Norway we are terrible drivers, but we know the roads and conditions. It's when the good drivers start coming that problems start. This one was an Austrian coach, and the road was blocked until twenty minutes ago. Of course, it's not conclusive. There may have been *fremmed folk*—what do you say?—people from outside here before the crash. What time do the gardeners go home, I wonder? Again, it could have been a local person. They sometimes come down here to the bar, I know. The road from Hardanger, too, was open . . . Still . . . it is interesting."

"What are you thinking?"

He raised his white-sandy eyebrows.

"That it seems to be narrowing itself rather to the people at the guest-house. You are thinking this as well as I."

I looked out on the shimmering oily-black and yellow of the water.

"You are forgetting the fjord," I said.

"We *never* forget the fjord," he said, emphatically. "But remember how exposed you are, travelling by water. Remember how people love to look out over water at the end of a fine day, at sunset, during the last light. There are rooms in the guest-house that surely overlook the water. Over on the island there, there are summer cottages—see, their lights are on at the moment. Anyone would be taking a most terrible risk."

I looked. Yes, even in twilight a murderer arriving by boat would feel horribly exposed . . . I said reluctantly:

"There is one more thing. The guest-house has a young man, a sort of odd-job man who turns himself to anything that needs doing so far as I can see. He was waiting at the end of the path that leads to the road most of the evening after dinner. He was supposed to be meeting guests off a bus. He would know if anyone came down the main path."

Stein Bjørhovde nodded contentedly.

"Again, you see."

"Oh, I *see* all right."

The fair man stood there, quiet as still water.

"Who exactly was in the guest-house tonight?"

I had already got that worked out in my mind.

"Of the house-staff, I can't say. Probably some went home after dinner—maybe all of them did. The proprietress was alone in the bar. Of the guests: there was a party of Germans—you spoke to one at the top of the path. There was an American family, apparently casual tourists.

And there was the romantic novelists' party. I can give you a list of them later, but there'd be about nine or ten. Of these, two had guests for dinner, who are still here. One was my sister—you saw her with her young man at the top. He was supposed to go back to Bergen on the last bus, but of course the accident prevented him."

"I see. And you know all these people?"

"All in the 'romantic party,' if that's the right description, though only on a casual basis."

"How well did you know—" he gestured with his hand towards the sodden pink bundle on the landing-stage.

"Very little. We met up on the boat from Newcastle—oh—three days ago. She is the sort of woman I fly from, and in the time since I've mostly flown. Still, we've inevitably come across each other now and again."

He thought.

"You are here to accompany your sister?"

"Yes. Just to get her over her first shyness. She's not used to these gatherings—though, God knows, neither am I." A touch of bravado entered my tone as I said: "I'm joining my wife at Oppheim tomorrow."

Stein Bjørhovde shook his head, and made a sound that I took to be a Norwegian "tut-tut."

"That is not possible. You know it is not possible." I put on my obstinate expression, a male version of Cristobel's party-piece. "You are one of the people at the guest-house. I have no reason to suspect you, but I have no reason to suspect any of the others either. I cannot just let you—" he waved his hand into the darkness—

"take off, because you are from Scotteland Eeyard."

I withdrew my obstinate expression, and sighed.

"No."

"On the other hand, if you would take the matter in hand . . ."

"How on earth can I take the matter in hand if I am a suspect?" I asked, exasperated.

"I mean only that you *blir med*, that you are with us, as we go along, helping, perhaps interpreting, even suggesting . . ."

"I am on holiday," I said.

"Of course we get authorization from your headquarters. No doubt you get time off as compensation . . ."

He seemed to think we had the same sort of working conditions as factory hands. Probably they did in Norway. I seemed to remember that when their navy was searching for a Russian submarine, they all knocked off on Sunday. It wasn't like that at the Eeyard.

"I don't know," I said. "I'd be in a very ambiguous position. I don't see what the alternative is . . ."

"Of course, to remain here, with the other . . . people," he concluded delicately. "Until the investigation is concluded. It is said, perhaps unfairly, that we in the Norwegian police work very, very slowly."

I looked at him, and he looked back with blue infinity in his eyes. I turned away from the body and we trudged up the hill.

7

The Secrets of the Bedroom

The natural place to start was Amanda's room, with the other rooms coming a good second. Most of them, luckily, were already vacated. Stein Bjørhovde stood on the lawn for a bit, organizing his subordinates to take preliminary statements from everybody staying, working or merely happening that evening to be at the guest-house. The ones they were primarily interested in, however, were obviously the English and American writers. Stein told them they could stay on the porch or in the lounge, but they should not go back to their rooms. The two policemen with the best English were given tables and chairs in the dining-room and in the bar, now closed, so that they could interview the conference delegates one by one. On my advice Stein despatched the most stalwart of his men to fetch down Lorelei Zuckerman, but to my surprise she came like a lamb.

As we stood there on the lawn, making last arrangements, the boy arrived from the road

with the new guests. At last the bus had got
through. Momentarily nonplussed, the proprietress darted inside, and within two minutes she
was out again, directing the boy to bring round
the guest-house car, and drive the guests to the
Kvalevåg Hotel. The situation was explained to
them, and at least two of the party expressed the
strongest determination to stay. The proprietress smiled a steely smile, and ushered them
into the car. They went.

So now Stein, Svein and I could go to Amanda's room, or invade her private sanctum as she
might have put it. I stood outside the door, almost nervous, as if she were still there to shout
"Come in" and then swallow me in pink. But I
knew she was not there: I had given mouth-to-
mouth to that sodden bundle of pink on the
landing-stage. I squared my shoulders, turned
the key in the door, and we all three trudged in.

The work divided itself up almost without our
discussing it. Stein and Svein took charge of all
the technical stuff—the fingerprinting and
whatnot—and began a thorough inspection of
clothes, bed, luggage and so on. I was happy to
leave that work to them, for Amanda had in the
few days she had been there left her imprint of
frilly self-regard on the otherwise almost Spartan room. I took on the little desk under the
windows, at which Amanda had presumably sat
to write the last pages that there ever would be
of *The Pretender's Sweetheart*, while looking
out, with deadly appropriateness, at the cherry
blossom that stood immediately under her window, in indecently full bloom.

In fact, there was no copy of the manuscript of *The Pretender's Sweetheart* on the desk, nor was it to be found in any of the drawers. I can't say I was very surprised. I couldn't see Amanda spending her holiday beavering away at romance-in-the-heather, whatever she might pretend. There was, in fact, no "work in progress" anywhere in the room. There were paperback copies of some of her earlier candy-floss dreadfuls, probably to be given away to any of her admirers in Norway who might happen to present themselves. I put them aside, to peruse them if absolutely necessary. I turned to the desk, and the writing that Amanda had really been engaged on.

The first thing that took my attention, on the right of the little desk, was the English draft of Amanda's letter to the editor of *Bergens Tidende*. It was, perhaps surprisingly, almost as short as she had claimed.

Dear Sir,

If my romantic novels are the trash Ms. Sørby claims them to be in her article, the logical deduction, in view of the millions who read me, is that women are idiots. Is this what Ms. Sørby believes?

Yours faithfully
Amanda Fairchild

Succinct and to the point. It was this letter that the boy had translated and posted at the box on the Bergen–Kvalevåg road while he waited for the bus. Two days later it appeared in the paper in an inconspicuous position, the editor not having realized whom it was from. Stein told me then that the boy had translated it into a virulent form of Nynorsk, which is apparently a sort of official dialect spoken mainly by peasants and university lecturers. I never found out whether he had done this as a joke, because that's what he spoke, or as some form of revenge.

That letter, though, was the one Amanda had written before dinner, and had translated immediately afterwards. How she had spent the time between her visit with me to the bar and her fatal visit to the boathouse was clear from the writing-pad in the centre of the desk. It contained letter paper of no great distinction which could have been obtained at any British stationer's. Though not exactly cheap paper, it was quite ordinary. The handwriting was the same as on the draft letter to *Bergens Tidende*, and was surely therefore Amanda's own. I took the letter carefully in my hand.

"That's odd," said Stein, rummaging in the wardrobe.

"What is?" I asked, tearing my attention away.

"Are you an expert on women's underwear?"

"I don't make a fetish of it."

"There seem to be two quite different types here. There's a lot of this—what would you call it?—frilly satin petticoats and . . . things, with lacy edges and all that . . ."

"Yes, I can see. Tired businessmen underwear."

"Is that what it is? For fairly old businessmen, I should think. Then there's some—not so much —perfectly sensible stuff: tights and pants and all that. My wife goes over and gets that sort of thing at your Marks and Spencers."

"Is the same thing noticeable with the ordinary clothes?"

Stein rummaged around.

"Yes, it is. Two quite different types of outfit. There's ordinary navy slacks, and thick shoes, and two or three heavy duty pullovers—they're old, too."

"Not bought specially. So if she was going on a walking holiday after these junketings are over, it looks as though that was something she had done before. Wait a minute—her travel folder may be here somewhere." I rummaged through the drawers and pigeonholes, which were surprisingly orderly, and came up with Amanda's folder. "Here we are. Yes—the conference ends on the twenty-second, and she isn't booked on the boat back to Newcastle until the twenty-ninth. Presumably she was going on somewhere else . . . though I can't see that the travel agent has booked anything for her . . ."

"OK," said Stein, putting back the clothes. "Probably going up into the mountains. Not interesting."

"Oh, I don't know," I said, frowning. "It could be . . ." But I couldn't formulate my thoughts, and I turned back to the letter in the centre of the desk.

Dearest Robbie,

You whispered before you "went your way" that it was wonderful to be together, to touch each other. Darling, *how* you summed up my thoughts! My eyes were so full that I couldn't see you, though I think you waved. I can only hope nobody saw. Because remember, love, that we *must* show care, *must* remember that I have a job to do, one that is very important to me, and that for the moment you don't fit in too well! *You* must see that!

So let's remember that we have a wonderful week ahead of us after the twenty-second, and try not to be together too much until then —both of us have so much on, so many people to meet, that that shouldn't be difficult.

By the way—tremendous fun!—I just got a note

But there the letter broke off. I read it through a second time, found it hardly less puzzling, and then looked towards Stein and Svein, who were pottering in and around Amanda's bed.

"Hey, listen to this," I said. "It's what she was writing just before she died."

When I had read it, Stein creased his brow.

"Some boyfriend or other. Someone who saw her off at Heathrow, and is joining her here after the conference."

"She came here by sea. It would have been Newcastle, or perhaps King's Cross. She didn't inflict herself on us till after the boat had sailed, so I didn't notice if anybody saw her off. But I don't think that quite squares with the letter anyway."

"Why not?"

"She says they must show care, and remember that she has a job to do. And she hopes nobody saw her tears. It reads as if what she's referring to is the days ahead—the remaining days of the conference. They must try not to be together too much until the twenty-second, she says, as they both have so much on. Obvious inference: she's writing to someone who's actually at the conference. Only when the conference is over can they really be themselves."

Stein came over and read it through again.

"Yes, it does hear like that—sound like that . . . Wait, I think there's a list of people at the conference by her bed . . ."

"Good. Look through it for all the Roberts. There certainly isn't one at the *Gjestgiveri*, but then, if there was, that wouldn't be whom she was writing to. Presumably she was either going to post it, or give it to him at tomorrow's session. It has to be someone staying somewhere else."

"Has there been any sign of a boyfriend?" asked Stein, going through the list and taking notes.

"None. It's all been totally professional so far: fans and fellow-writers, publishers and critics. There hasn't been anyone, that I've seen, with whom Amanda had a personal relationship. And however much she may have liked men, they didn't flock round her, of course."

"Why, 'of course'?" Stein asked.

"You never encountered Amanda's manner.

It died with her. Men didn't flock around her because she put them off. It was a manner—if we may generalize about the sexes—that would tend to make men cringe. Especially today. The feminist movement has all but destroyed that manner. I noticed the chap from Kenya seemed to be able to put up with it, but it may be he is more used to it: in a place like that the whites would probably be thirty or forty years behind the current ways of behaving. No, Amanda certainly had conversations with men—fellow writers like Arthur Biggs, for example—but there never seemed anything but a purely professional interest in them: it was all about sales, contracts and such-like, even when she talked to Wes Mackay, the Kenyan. Right—what candidates have you got for 'Robbie' there?"

"Someone called Robert Lefebre—address in Lyons, France. One called Robert Achinowuba, address in Lagos—"

"That'd be the one with the robes."

"Then there's a Robert Macintosh, from St. Andrews, a Robin Grant—should we count a Robin?—"

"Oh, sure."

"—from Ontario, and a Robert Christopherson from Iowa. That's it. I suppose the Canadian, the American and the Scot are the most likely."

I shrugged.

"Most likely, yes. But we can't rule out any of them. The point is, we know nothing or next to nothing about Amanda's past. So anything is possible."

" 'Next to nothing?' So something you do know?"

"Only what I gleaned from *Happy Tears*—a history of the romantic love story, written by one Arthur Biggs, who is here in the guest-house, so you will certainly meet him. He has a short biographical dictionary of writers in the back, from which I gleaned that she was a West Country girl, became an actress, had a less than dazzling career, and took to writing candy-floss romances. More than that I know not. Except that, at the moment, she is extremely successful —or *was*, up to an hour or two ago. Which brings up the question of who is to inherit . . . You could get on to the Yard about that, or I can . . . Now, is there anything we haven't—"

But even as I spoke, I was surprised to hear soft footsteps from outside, on the landing. *Soft* footsteps. The policemen Stein had with him were mostly lean, some to the point of gaunt-ness, but they were tall and capable-looking. They would not be soft on their feet, if they were walking naturally, and why should they go softly? The guests were all supposed to be wait-ing downstairs in the lounge, or giving their ac-counts of the evening to the policemen in the bar or in the dining-room. Who, then, was out-side on the landing? The proprietress?

I walked quickly but silently to the door, and opened it. At the other end of the corridor, about to put his key in his bedroom door, was Arthur Biggs. He started guiltily. I did not put too much weight on that start. People who sud-denly find themselves involved in a murder case are always starting guiltily, even if they've been caught doing nothing worse than pouring themselves a cup of coffee.

"Mr. Biggs?" I said, my voice raised. The hand with the key in it fell back to his side. "I thought it was agreed that all the guests should stay downstairs in the lounge?"

"Well, yes," he said, his voice taking on a touch of the querulous, now he was no longer in command. "But I didn't realize we were supposed to regard it as an *order*."

I walked down the corridor and stood by him. A natural and unpleasant confidence was fighting in his expression and in the set of his shoulders to get the better of a nasty bout of nerves.

"How did you get here? There was a policeman on duty at the bottom of the stairs."

Arthur Biggs turned and pointed to an opening labelled EMERGENCY STAIRS and NØDUTGANG, coming out almost opposite his room—a poky, dark, uninviting well of stairs.

"They come out just outside the kitchens. I always investigate these things, in case of fire—terrible risk, in an old wooden building like this. The policeman in the lounge was occupied in getting something for Lorelei Zuckerman, so I slipped out and came up."

"Then clearly you *did* realize it was an order that you stayed in the lounge." I looked at him sternly, and he dropped his eyes. "What did you want to get from your room?"

Now he seemed to regain confidence. Perhaps his mission was entirely innocent.

"I wanted my notepad. It's obvious we're in

for a long session tonight. I thought I'd use the time mapping out a good-sized piece on Amanda as romance writer—maybe for the *Sunday Express*."

"I see. And maybe a little human interest piece on how you found yourself caught up in her murder?"

He looked cunning, as if I'd tried to catch him out.

"The word 'murder' hasn't been mentioned yet. Not to us ordinary mortals. Among ourselves, of course . . . But, yes, I *did* think that, if it *did* turn out to be murder, the *Daily Grub* might be interested in a personal account—"

"You want to get in first?"

He spread out his hands in an Anglo-Gallic gesture.

"What's wrong with that? And an on-the-spot account does have a special thrill for readers."

"And you think that Amanda is—was—of sufficient interest to the general public for the *Grub* people to make you a whopping offer?"

"Yes, I do. And if she hadn't been before, she would be now. A dead writer is always a best-selling one. Have you ever seen a news hoarding reading FAIRLY-WELL-SELLING NOVELIST DIES? But actually Amanda *was* of interest to the general public in any case."

"I'd never heard of her before I came here."

"That, if you'll pardon my saying so, is neither here nor there. You grew up in a somewhat rarefied literary atmosphere. I am talking about the general public. Amanda appeared on things like *TV-am* and *The Wogan Show*. For years she

was one of the panellists on *The Petticoat Line*."
He saw me shudder, and said nastily: "Oh, I
realize you're a Radio Three man, and probably
only watch the news and *Mastermind* on the
box. But I assure you the general public not only
read her in enormous numbers, they knew her
as a personality as well. She did a lot of 'personal
appearance' things as well—opening supermarkets, housing projects, bazaars. She was kept
very busy."

"So it seems," I said, watching him. "Quite
apart from the writing."

"Yes," said Arthur Biggs. "Quite apart from
the writing."

"If she did, in fact, write the books that appeared over her name," I continued.

"Quite," said Arthur Biggs.

8

Deadly Deception

I took the key from his hand, unlocked his door, and went into his bedroom. There was a blank exercise book on his desk, and I took it up and waved it at him.

"This do?"

He nodded, rather stiff and on his dignity.

"We shall be going over this room later anyway," I pointed out to him. "We have to be sure that no one else has gone over it first." I led the way out on to the landing, and locked the door behind me. After a second's thought I returned to him the key. "You'd better come along to Amanda's room," I said, and he trotted after me with a new access of confidence, or self-importance. It didn't take much, I mused, either to deflate or reflate him.

"I think you'd better hear this," I said to Stein and Svein, leading Briggs into Amanda's sanctum. They sat down on the bed, looking mystified.

"Of course, I don't *know*," Arthur Briggs began, nervously, his hands gesturing spasmodically as he suddenly found himself at the centre of attention. "It's just as much a guess on my part as it is on yours."

"My guess was made on the basis of your book," I pointed out.

"Yes, I realize that. I saw you had a copy on the bus today."

He said it as if I had earned myself a good mark.

"As soon as I sat down and thought about it, you'd made it pretty clear there," I said. "Why did you do that—as a sort of joke?"

I looked at him. Lorinda Mason, as he was known to his limited circle of readers, didn't look the sort to make jokes. He was below middle height, physically unimpressive, with a sandy moustache that was more apologetic than assertive, and weak, bottle-blue eyes. He looked like a bank clerk who would never make it to manager. But there was about the man this ineffable air of self-importance, and when I suggested a joke he seemed to wiggle, metaphorically, in his nether regions.

"Something of the kind," he agreed. "Of course, people are always making jokes about romance writers, and the whopping errors they make—"

"Not you, I'm sure," I said cunningly, and watched his face to see the ever-present self-esteem turn up the edges of his mouth. On cue it came.

"One does have a *cer*tain pride in one's work," he murmured. "But one gets all too used to other writers who simply won't take the trouble. There are plenty of errors of that sort in Amanda's books. But what made me sit up was the one that you obviously noticed."

"That someone born in Tiverton should imagine Exeter was in Somerset," I said.

"Quite. A Devonian knows his own county town. Though if you look at the text closely it wasn't *quite* as definite as that. One could *just* take it that they were looking *from* the tower out to the Somerset hills in the distance."

"Can one?" I asked.

"I've no idea. But anyway, I can't see a Devon girl writing that, can you? She would make it quite unambiguous. That was an early book I quoted from: I suspect the publishers—and Amanda herself, probably—have got a lot more careful in recent ones. In the early days there were five or six Amanda Fairchild titles a year. Now there are only two. I imagine she always reads them, because nowadays she has to do an awful lot of chatting to fans, and suchlike, and she'd have to know what she is supposed to have written. When the early ones came out they must have been too busy establishing her public persona and managing the publicity machine to take the elementary precaution of having her read all the stuff that appeared under her name."

"Was that," asked Stein, "the point of it all?"

"I would imagine so," I said. "Do you know anything more?" I asked, turning to Arthur Biggs.

"*Know?* Certainly not. But one might *guess.*

Her publishers are the Tamworth group. Enormous group, enormous list, rather soulless. It's a perfectly good list, but they've never had any personalities on it, not in the romance field. They've had nobody who could rival, say, Cartland in putting herself over to the public. Until Amanda, that is. In fact, a lot of their romance writers have always been men, and we do suffer from a disability in this field." He made a self-deprecatory gesture, but somehow it managed to imply that, were he otherwise sexed, he would be an absolute wow on the chat shows. "And even with the women—well, as you will have noticed since you've been here, as often as not romance writers are perfectly mousy little creatures, with not an atom of self-projection."

"Just doing it for the money?" asked Svein.

"Yes. Because if you can strike the right note, the money is certainly there, the market never fails. But some of them of course, are also acting out their romantic fantasies. Like your sister," he said as an afterthought, nodding to me. I suspect that pinprick was his mean little revenge.

"I don't know where that leaves you," I said.

"Oh—in it for the money, purely for the £.s.d. I came from crime—there's no money there at all. Anyway, granted that Tamworth had an absolute preponderance of the male and mousy, it must have occurred to someone that if they wanted to get some figure on their list to rival the Sugar-Plum Queen, they'd better hire one. And hire an actress rather than a writer—one who would put on a marvellous *show*."

"And the collected works would be written by

the males and the mousies. But what would they have to say about *that*?"

"Why should they mind? If you are a born mouse, all this publicity stuff is sheer torment anyway. And if their books sold twice, three times what they would under their own name, they certainly wouldn't begrudge a percentage going to Amanda, who was up there doing her outrageous bit on the box, or being interviewed by ghastly women for the women's pages of newspapers."

"Amanda," I said, "begins to make a lot more sense."

"In what way?" asked Stein.

"She was very near—mean—with money. I assumed it was the equivalent of John Paul Getty installing pay telephones, but probably the real reason was that she didn't have that much."

"She was always interested in contracts," contributed Arthur Biggs. "It always amused me that she had to hold back on her *real* interest—her percentage."

"Then there was the problem of how intelligent she really was," I went on. "It bewildered me—I never could make up my mind. Out of the blue you'd hear evidence of a sharp mind: that letter to the editor about the Sørby woman's article, in fact all her arguments with her. Whether you agreed with her or not, she managed her side very cleverly. She spotted things, she sized up people. But then she'd come out with some appalling piece of marshmallow silliness, and all sorts of dated garbage about the sexes, the sort of crap you wouldn't expect to read in a Victorian novel of any pretensions, It wasn't that she was ever inconsistent in any pin-downable way, but somehow things never entirely cohered."

"So you think she was *hired* to put on a performance as a romantic writer?" asked Stein. "To *be* what people expected?"

"I think so," said Arthur Biggs.

"But that it often conflicted with her real character," I added. "Think of the first night here. There was Lorelei Zuckerman putting on this incredible performance—another performance? or just her uniquely horrible self?—anyway, the general reaction of most of us as dinner was ending was to crawl away and die, right? And la Zuckerman gave the impression that she would be delighted if we did. But it was Amanda who insisted on coming over, greeting her and screwing a few words out of her. It was—and I don't use the word lightly—extremely brave. It also showed an acute understanding of character and occasion. But it did *not* go with the froth and the silliness and the 'look at little me' of her general performance."

"No, it didn't," agreed Arthur Biggs.

"Or—turning the telescope round—the sort of intelligence she showed when she took on this Sørby creature didn't gell with the kind of woman who made all sorts of appalling howlers in her books. If *that* Amanda hadn't known when the railways came in, she'd have gone away and looked it up. A lot of people aren't sure when photography was invented, but they tend to put it later than it was rather than earlier, unless they are the historical equivalent of illiterate. And that I am quite sure Amanda wasn't. She would *not* have a Regency heroine clutching a snapshot. So, if Biggs is right we can now recognize all the contradictions for what they were—bad co-ordination—and start building up a picture of the real Amanda."

We all thought about that for a moment, and then Svein, the sergeant, said: "If it was the *real* Amanda who got herself killed."

I thought this was a brilliant remark, and shot him an appreciative glance. But I didn't want to indulge in any really vital discussion so long as the inquisitive and self-important Arthur Biggs was there. I turned to him.

"Right. Well—is there anything further you can tell us about Amanda Fairchild?"

He thought, conspicuously.

"I don't think so. We met now and then, at conferences such as this one. We had no social contacts beyond that, though we may have talked at the odd publisher's party, I think . . . No, I can't think of anything else I could tell you."

"We shall in any case be talking to you, probably tomorrow," I said, escorting him to the door.

"I have told everything I know to the chap downstairs," he protested.

"Quite," I said calmly. "And we'll be going over it again with you in due course. Just a matter of routine. Thank you for your help. Oh, and Mr. Biggs—this time stay down there in the lounge as you were asked to, eh?"

He slunk off, and I watched him down the main stairs. No doubt the policeman at the bottom would find a few well-chosen words to say to him in one or other language before he would be allowed to get down to writing his think-piece on Amanda Fairchild for the *Sunday Express*.

"Are they all like that?" asked Stein.

"There is infinite variety—you'll see," I promised. "One in particular . . ."

"The lady with the name like a siren?" enquired Svein.

"Quite. Known to her readers as Lorelei le Neve, which has a double implication of *femme fatale*. Whether, and in what sense, she has been *fatale* in this case—"

We were interrupted by a tap on the door, and a young constable handed over a sheaf of papers. I gathered it was notes from the preliminary interviews downstairs.

"Are they finished?" I asked, surprised.

"All but about three or four," said Stein. "I suspect the constable is trying to tell us that the people in the lounge are beginning to complain. He is a foolish young man. He should realize that they are foreigners, and can't stand on their rights since they don't know them. They will have to wait. In any case, the interviews are not finished yet. I gather they are having trouble with a Finn."

"That figures," I said. "He's a drunk of world class. I suggest that what you'll have to do if you want to get any sense out of him is lock him in his room overnight. And don't do like the BBC did with Brendan Behan."

"Who was he?"

"A playwright in his spare time. The BBC managed to lock him in a room, accidentally on purpose, for a couple of hours before he was due to be interviewed. They thought it would make sure he was sober. Innocent little things they must have been at the BBC in those days. They should have frisked him before they locked him in. That interview was one of the best things the BBC ever put out, but sobriety had nothing to do with it. So frisk the man before you lock him in, and go through the room beforehand with spare halves of vodka very much in mind. Because he could just be a key witness."

"Why?"

"I suspect that for much of the vital period that we're interested in, there were four together in one room—or one suite. So there will probably be a question of their alibi-ing each other."

"Would he have been sober at the time?" asked Stein.

"No," I admitted.

"Then I doubt if he will be of any use," Svein said. "I have much experience of drunks."

Judging by what I had seen of Bergen, even early in the afternoon, he spoke no less than the truth.

"Still, at some stage he has got to be interviewed when he's sober," I protested. "You might try him sober, then let him have two or three and try him again. A comparison of the two interviews might be instructive—might even provide material for an article in the *Norwegian Police Gazette*, if there's any such thing."

Stein stirred. He felt we should be working.

"Right! Now let's try a lightning tour through the other bedrooms. I'll get as many of my men as I can from downstairs, and we'll do all the obvious things and then let them go to bed."

I think we would have been less solicitous at the Yard about the suspects getting a good night's sleep. Still, I went along with him, because he was in charge. We all left and locked Amanda's room, and began a fast but systematic going-through of all the other bedrooms. I left Stein and Svein to do mine and Cristobel's. All the others I assisted in—looking for "paper" evidence more than anything else, but obviously not shutting my eyes to other things as well. At the end of an hour and a half's gruelling labour, the points I had thought worthy of inclusion in my notebook were:

Three books by Amanda in Lorelei Zuckerman's room, all apparently bought at the conference stall.

No clothes wet around the sleeves or knees, as might be expected after drowning someone.

Every single author brought with him copies of his own books, even (Stein told me) Cristobel.

Every single romantic writer had his quota of duty-free grog stashed away in or on top of his wardrobe.

We gathered at the top of the stairs, and by a mere nod of the head we decided to call it a day. I looked down over the banisters to where the assembled guests and some of the staff were sitting round on the peasant sofas and peasant easy chairs. Every one of them was aware of our presence on the landing; not one of them looked up at us. They were all very quiet, some reading, a couple writing, some just sitting there. Cristobel and Bernard were the only ones who had any contact with each other. They were in adjacent chairs, holding hands.

Before we descended I said to Stein in a low voice:

"When you get back to the Bergen Station, I think you should telex her publishers. Tamworth, the name was. Say something like: 'Amanda Fairchild murdered. Will ring her editor ten a.m.' We need to find out if what Arthur Biggs suggested is anything more than a conjecture."

Stein nodded, and we proceeded down into the lounge. When he said "You are all free now to go to bed," his announcement acted as a catalyst. Everybody started talking at once, there was nervous laughter, Arthur Biggs collected his little knot of supporters around him to bolster him up, and only Lorelei Zuckerman began at once to act on Stein's permission, heaving herself painfully from her chair, and being helped gradually up the stairs by Felicity Maxwell.

Stein had one thing to do before leaving. As Lorelei toiled step by step upwards, he spoke to his toughest-looking sergeant. When he had done, the man went over to Martti Whatever-it-was, the Finn, comatose in his corner chair. He rapidly and efficiently frisked him as he lay there, and handed to a waiting constable an empty half of vodka. Then he heaved the man to his feet, and, satisfied that Lorelei was by now in her suite, he began the laborious process of getting him upstairs. Eventually we heard, from a distance, the sound of protesting bedsprings as Martti was thrown on to them, and then the locking of a door. I hoped they'd been damned thorough in their search of his room.

Stein left two of his men on guard, and I went out on to the porch to see him off.

"We'll discuss all the forensic stuff tomorrow," he said in his laconic way. Then they drove off.

When I went back into the lounge, people were beginning to disperse upstairs. The proprietress and the boy-in-waiting were standing around, obviously willing everyone to stand not upon the order of their going but go at once. I went over to Cristobel, who was standing by the bottom of the stairs.

"Are you all right now, Chris?"

She nodded.

"Yes, I'm much better . . . But I still feel awfully frightened."

"That's all right," I said reassuringly. "There's

still a camp bed in my room left over from Jan's stay. You can sleep there with me."

Cristobel said, "Oh, thank you, Perry." Was it my imagination, or did she say it with rather less warmth than I had expected? Bernard, like Everard Manning, was being accommodated in one of the rooms prepared for the new arrivals of that evening. Could it have been that she had been intending to spend the night with quite another male protector?

No doubt I had blundered again. But really—could I be expected to know the sexual habits of renegade monks?

9

The Puppet-Master

Breakfast next morning was a curious meal.
Cristobel and I were down early, neither of us
having slept well. We sat at the end of one of the
long tables, but as others came down in ones and
twos they all sat some way away from us—farther down, or at the other table. Even Maryloo
Parker avoided us. When we went up to the
serving table for refills—and Cristobel went
very frequently, since the murder seemed to
have done nothing to satisfy that Girl Guide's
appetite—they smiled nervously at us, then
bent down to look intently at the cold pork or
the little tins of pickled herring. Well away from
us they conversed very differently from their
usual high-voiced mode of communication—
they leant forward and used hushed tones, occa-
sionally looking down the table at me. They
might have been Victorians discussing the private life of the Prince of Wales. I had no doubt
that it was I rather than Cristobel who was the
problem. Later they would no doubt milk Chris

for all she was worth (and she was highly milk-able). But I had changed, for all of them—no matter how innocent they knew themselves to be. I was on the other side.

Eventually Bernard came down and sat with us. Apparently he hadn't slept well either, and he looked ragged. He said he had difficulty coping with death, which suggested he was right to leave the monastery. He toyed with a slice of wholemeal bread and a sliver of pseudo-Swiss cheese, and I rather guessed that he and Chris would rather I was gone. I downed my second cup of coffee and went. As I closed the door, the volume of noise from conversation inside rose appreciably.

Upstairs everything was quiet. I had rather thought the Finn might be howling for spirituous liquor, but all was still. "Sleeping it off," said the sergeant outside his room, winking knowingly. He pointed to a room farther along the corridor, where he said Bjørhovde and Jernsletten were already at work. From the other direction I could hear that the technical boys were still going over Amanda's room. It was all comfortingly familiar in the midst of strangeness, like tuning into the BBC in a Moscow hotel.

Stein had not much to tell me, but he said he hoped to have something from the scientific mob in the course of the morning. In the meanwhile, he presumed that I would be the one to ring Amanda's publisher. There was a room at the end of the corridor which was empty, and which he had commandeered: it was for VIPs, and its telephone had an automatic line out independent of the guest-house exchange. He had arranged that all calls from there would be charged to the police. Would there be anybody at the publisher's office yet?

"Nobody of any consequence, I should imagine," I said. "Britain is an hour behind, remember. But I can at least try to make contact."

"I'll show you where. Then Svein and I will interview the Finn."

We located the bedroom together, and I paused in the doorway as Stein and Svein went back to the Finn's room. Stein took out the skeleton key, but as he inserted it in the lock there arose from inside the room the sound of a bass-baritone voice. What it was singing I did not know, but it sounded like the nearest approach to an aria in one of those gigantic Finnish operas based on the *Kalevala*. It certainly boded no good for Stein.

"If you keep him there long enough under supervision," I pointed out comfortingly, "he's just got to run out." I tactfully refrained from pointing out that they could try brushing up their techniques of room-searching.

Stein had researched the number, and I got straight through to London. As usual with international calls, I got a line much clearer than anything one was likely to meet with on day-to-day business within the London area. There was someone in at the Tamworth offices, though she was breathless, as if she had just arrived. She told me that Amanda Fairchild's editor would be Auberon Lawrence, who did all the Romance, but she did very much doubt whether he would be in yet. She'd ring around and get back to me. Ringing from Norway, did I say? Well, she wouldn't be a moment.

"It's very odd," she said, when she came back on my line, "but he seems to be on the way to Norway himself."

"Good God," I said, "that was quick."

"Apparently he came in last night after a party, to get something he'd forgotten. He's a little bit—well—fey. He left a note in the Chairman's office, or rather on the door. It's not too coherent, I'm afraid, but it seems that he found a telex message from Norway—would that be from you?"

"Yes," I said.

"Anyway, it seems that he got straight on to the airports and found there was a charter flight to Oslo at eight-thirty, with a spare seat. He's on that, will change planes there, and fly on to Bergen. Does that make sense to you? If the connection holds, he will be there by about eleven-twenty."

"Great," I said. "I'll try and meet him there."

"Is there anything *wrong*?" the telephonist asked.

"You could say so. Amanda Fairchild is dead."

"Oh no! And I'm sitting here reading her latest. No more of those *lovely* books!"

It was my first contact with an Amanda fan. She had sounded very sensible, too.

I begged a police car off Stein, and set off for Bergen airport, a bit nervously, driving on the wrong side of the road and sitting on the wrong side of the car. The combination of pot-holes and hairpin bends over dizzying drops did nothing for my confidence, but forty minutes later I got there. Bergen airport was pretty much like any other—cleaner, perhaps, but greyer. It was full of people in drab clothes drinking black coffee and eating horrible-looking cream cakes. At the news-stand they had a copy of that morning's *Times*, and I sat over a cup of disgraceful tea, reading about the terminal gasps of the Thatcher government.

When the 11:05 Oslo–Bergen plane disgorged its load, it was easy to spot the passengers who were English. They were less good-looking than the others. Which of the five or six was likely to prove an English publisher I was less than sure, but for safety's sake I had had a message sent through to the plane that I would be waiting at the barrier. In the event it was a cherubic little man, with thinning hair and bloodshot eyes, who looked as if, at better times in his life, he might be utterly charming, but who for the moment was not finding it easy to gather his mental equipment together. Under his right eye there was a tic in his cheek, perhaps caused by all the happy tears that must have flowed down it. He soon got over his surprise at being met by a Scotland Yard man, and took me as a matter of course.

"Thought I'd better come," he said, in a high-pitched, aristocratic squeak, as he trotted beside me towards the car.

"Good of you. I wasn't at all expecting it."

"Difficult matter. Ticklish," he said.

"For you, yes."

"More than you can know," he insisted.

"Oh, I think I may have some idea," I said complacently, but he was wrapped up in the contemplation of the ticklishness of it all, and didn't notice.

"To think I very nearly came on this binge *anyway*," he said fretfully. "We sent someone from our Australian subsidiary instead, but now I rather wish I had done. I don't suppose it would have made any difference, but it would have saved me all this hassle."

"Quite," I said. "Particularly as no one would ever suspect you of killing off one of your best golden-egg layers. What put you off? The thought of the company you'd have to keep?"

"No, no. Not at all. *Charm*ing people . . . many of them. No, it was more the thought of the sessions. I do trust I've missed 'Whither the Gothic?' "

"You have."

"Whither went it?"

"I rather think it proved to be more of a stationary than a mobile vehicle," I said. I let us into the car, but before driving off I had a thought. "I wonder if Kvalevåg is the best place to take you. I want a long, quiet chat, and the place is packed tight with guests and police."

He shrugged, and looked around him bleakly.

"Somewhere quiet where I can have a nice pick-me-up or two. Do you know, there was no alcoholic refreshment on the plane from Oslo?"

"Perhaps we could go to the Scandilux. It's where the conference is being held, but it has one or two tiny little bars where no one seems to go."

"So long as you don't *pitch*fork me into a session. What is it this morning? Second chance romances?"

"As a matter of fact, I rather think it is."

He put on an air of world-weariness.

"Most of the women that read them, you know, have either never had a first chance, or else they've taken all too many!"

He was settling down as if for a snooze, so I braked suddenly to wake him up.

"On the way, I suggest I tell you exactly what happened to Amanda," I said.

"Yes—I suppose you must. If it's not something that can be hushed up altogether—" he looked at me hopefully, and I shook my head— "then I hope it was some sort of *beautiful* murder, something with glamour or passion in it. So that our publicity people can make something of it."

"Not a very beautiful death at all, I'm afraid," I said, remembering the sodden bundle of pink on the wooden slats. "And there was more than a touch of the ludicrous about it."

And through his sighs, I gave him a reasonably full account of Amanda's last evening, and her end. This took us all the way into Bergen, and then I had to concentrate on getting us both to the Scandilux. Fortunately Håkonshallen, farther along the promontory, was well signposted, so I made it with no major errors, and put the police car in the hotel parking basement with a sense of relief. When I turned off the ignition I found that Auberon Lawrence was unbeautifully asleep.

I jogged him into a sense of where and who he was, and we took a lift up to the hotel proper. I nosed out the dark, deserted little bar that I had noticed earlier in the week. There was not a soul there except a doleful barman reading a sociology textbook. I gracefully let Auberon buy me a drink, and watched delightedly as he held out his hand for the barman to take what he required, only to find that he extracted from his palm almost all the money he had changed at Fornebu airport. He took his terribly dry martini and I took my Scotch to a corner table, and we settled over our glasses as if they were pans of gold-dust.

"There's something I ought to tell you about Amanda," began Auberon Lawrence. Did he like people to call him "Bron," I wondered?

"That she didn't write the books published under her name?" I asked.

He gave an outraged squeak.

"Collapse of stout party!" he shrilled. He comforted himself at his glass, and that made him much brighter. "Of course! It's not a disaster. You've been reading that awful little stoat's awful little book."

"Arthur Biggs? Yes, I have."

"I suppose it's a wonder more people haven't picked it up. Luckily the two things are separated—one in the text, one in the biographical index. Anyway, people who read romantic novels don't read books *about* the romantic novel—they just go on reading more romantic novels. Luckily for us, I expect *Happy Tears* only sold to libraries, and then mainly on its title . . . May the appalling Biggs rot in hell for the ghastly little turd he is," he added, in his seraphic voice.

"Hadn't you better tell me about the whole business?" I suggested gently.

"Ah! Yes . . . well . . . Let's see, it began in, I think, 1965 or 6. Before my time, but not *much* before it. It was old Fothergill's idea, and I became his deputy in 1967, so if I wasn't in on the ground floor, I was certainly in at the first. What he was after was someone we could promote, make into a minor national figure. And all we had was—well—"

"Mousies?"

"Drearies, I'd call them. And more than half of them men. I don't want to get into this sex-grudge business—you know, 'Anything you can do I can't do half as well because I'm the wrong sex.' But promotion *is* easier in this game if you're a woman. The Americans are doing rather well at the moment with a romantic writer who looks like Gary Hart, but how many writers look like Gary Hart?"

"How many politicians?"

"Anyway, what old Fothergill decided was that the writers we had were perfectly good, so the easiest thing was to stick with the writers, but hire somebody as the front figure—somebody who could conform to every expectation the great romance-reading public has of the romantic writer. He hit on the idea of a not-too-successful actress who would settle for a regular, fairly modest income, in return for a lifetime of public performance. He came up with Amanda —with Maureen, rather, as she was then called —and the results were fabulous."

"I knew Amanda, but what sort of person was Maureen?"

"Ah—that's a difficult one. I knew Maureen, you see, quite early on. Used to wine and dine her if old Fothergill was busy; in fact, I took over the whole impersonation from quite an early stage. What was she like then? As I remember, quite commonsensical, businesslike, liked everything cut and dried and insisted on a price-tag on everything she did. A little bit actressy, if you know what I mean, but that didn't go amiss as far as the Amanda performance was concerned."

"You talk as if she was someone you *once* knew."

He thought.

"Yes . . . It's difficult to explain. It's not quite that she *became* Amanda, though there was an element of that. It's just that she became Amanda at our meetings. They were more or less public—at restaurants, at launching parties, television studios—and in places like that the performance had become second nature to her. Early on, when nobody would recognize her, she could be herself, but not any longer. No doubt she could still be herself with the publicity department. They got together periodically to discuss the details of her performance: what she would appear on, what she would open, the clothes she would wear. No doubt those discussions were completely businesslike, and she was still Maureen Shottery for them. As for me, I sometimes caught a glimpse of the 'real' person, but it was only a glimpse."

"And nobody ever guessed?"

He did a mental shuffle.

"Well . . . hardly anyone . . ."

"Arthur Biggs?"

"That horrible little creep. You saw what he put in that book of his . . ."

"Was it in fact a sort of blackmail?"

"Put bluntly, yes. Only it never was put bluntly. It was in fact the most genteel sort of pressurizing, never remotely acknowledged as such. He was with an utterly insignificant publisher called Robertson Harty, and he wanted to get on to our lists . . . Of course he became one of our authors."

"He didn't tell me that. He mentioned you quite objectively, as if you were nothing to him in the world."

"He was trying to fool you. Lorinda Mason, as he calls himself, is one of our middling-to-low earners, churning out three or four a year. He/she doesn't disgrace our list, but he's certainly no money-spinner."

"He never wrote any of the Amanda Fairchild books?"

"Oh no. We'd want someone with a much lighter touch than Arthur Biggs."

"Who did write them? Lots of people, or just one or two?"

"Recently just one or two. One of them does a conventional one—*Mood Indigo* is the next—

and the other either does a Second Chance or a Historical. I've just got a manuscript from her."

"*The Pretender's Sweetheart*?" I asked.

"How did you—? Oh—Amanda preparing the way, I suppose. That was the marvellous thing about Amanda: you could send her anywhere and be quite sure she'd do a marvellous job." A thought struck him. "I say—I *won*der how many manuscripts we could say she left behind completed?"

"That's if the whole business of the imposture doesn't have to come out at a trial," I pointed out.

He nodded gloomily.

"Getting a new performance on the road is going to take so long! And if it does all come out, who is going to trust us again?"

"You were saying that two people write as Amanda Fairchild now," I said, steering him back to the main point. "Is either of them here at the conference?"

"Oh no—shrinking violets, both of them."

"What about in the past? When you were putting out several Amanda Fairchild titles a year?"

"Oh—masses of people. We used whatever seemed suitable, provided their authors consented. And it was very much worth their while to. Quite a few people would have had one or two under the Fairchild name. There are about eighty or ninety titles, you know."

"I know. Could you get me a full list of every writer whose work you used?"

His voice rose to a stratospheric squeak, like

Florence Foster Jenkins attempting the Queen of the Night.

"My dear man! Absolutely impossible! It's years ago!"

"But couldn't you get someone back in London to go through the records?"

"Dear chap, there's *nothing* so scrappy and disorganized as publishers' records! We had to move five or six years ago, after we'd nearly been taken over by a dreadful Australian. I've no doubt most of the relevant stuff would have been jettisoned then."

"But your accounts department? They'd have to keep records because they pay the royalties."

"After they've been out of print for a couple of years, people reclaim their rights. We very seldom reprint old ones, unless it was a *very* popular title. People want to read the *latest* Amanda Fairchild, not something published way back in the 'sixties."

"I shouldn't have thought it made a great deal of difference," I said, but I put aside the idea since it seemed to reduce him to a quivering jelly. "Well, please do any checking you can. Meanwhile I suppose I can assume any of the British writers here might have contributed an Amanda Fairchild title?"

He shrugged.

"I suppose so. *Not* Arthur Biggs. Otherwise . . ."

"Or American? Would that be conceivable?"

"Could be. One or two with an American setting could quite easily be incorporated into the

Fairchild *oeuvre*. Quite a lot of our readers seem quite to like the idea of the place. They think it has glamour—if only they knew! In the early stages of the game we put in anything that seemed likely to go."

He was getting a bit pop-eyed, and was looking regretfully at his glass. I didn't have anything more to ask him, and didn't think his company alone was worth the Norwegian price for a drink.

"I must be getting back," I said. "They should be serving lunch upstairs. A very good cold table, with a glass of wine. Two if you're clever. I should think you could count as a substitute delegate." He had jumped up enthusiastically. "If you can stand the company, that is."

"Dear chap, the company's all in a day's work. Charming people, many of them, and they talk no more tosh than most other sorts of writer. Lead me to it!"

In fact I took him into the foyer and directed him to the fifth floor via the lifts. He bounced into one, with every appearance of lively anticipation. As I turned and headed towards the swing doors, through which I could see Bryggen and the wharfs drenched in sunlight, I suddenly got the most curious sensation, from the corner of my eye, of being watched. I stopped and turned in the direction the feeling came from, but saw nothing but a skirt disappearing up a staircase. I waited, looking around, but nobody seemed to be taking any notice of me whatever. I shook my head, dissatisfied, and went out into the sunlight, to walk off the whisky before I got back into the driving seat of the police car. Had I but known it, I was already over the Norwegian legal limit.

10

Attendants on the Queen

When I got back to Kvalevåg, negotiating the
Norwegian roads with a confidence born of a
little experience and a little alcohol, the first
person I saw there was Wes Mackay. He was
walking around the circular patch of lawn in
front of the house, but he was looking up to the
mountains on one side, or out to the fjord on the
other, as if he were itching to be away from the
petty irritant of murder, to become part of The
Big Outdoors.

As very probably he was. I sat in the driving
seat for a moment, fiddling with road maps, and
looking at him as if for the first time—looking at
him, in fact, in the light of a suspect. He certainly, at first glance, impressed one principally
as an outdoors man: no more than average
height, but broad, tough and capable. I guessed
him to be a bit over forty. The face was mous-
tached, to give it that slight look of Hemingway
that outdoors people seem to cultivate, though
why they should wish to look like that appalling

phoney is beyond me. In the case of Wes Mackay, the rugged image, the feeling that he had in his time taken on lions single-handed, was complicated by the fact that for a living he wrote sentimental love stories. But then so did Ernest Hemingway.

I got out of the police car and went over to him.

"How go things?"

He pulled at his bushy brown moustache.

"Pretty jumpy. That's why I came out to get a breath of air. The police want us to stay around the house, but the gardens are still within bounds. Except for the boathouse, but that's one place I don't feel like visiting anyway."

"I can understand that. I expect they'll restrict you for a day or two, and then you'll be free to do pretty much as you like." I added cunningly: "Especially you four in Lorelei Zuckerman's room. You ought to be able to alibi each other, put everyone in the clear."

Wes Mackay shrugged.

"Pretty much, maybe. Tell you the truth, I'd thought of doing a little experimenting in how long it would take to get from her room or from the bar, down to the boathouse, murder the poor woman, and then get back. But the thought of how *that* would look to the cops if they came upon me holds me back. They're pretty sure to do their own experiments anyway."

"Sure to. So you weren't *all* in her room *all* the time until you heard about the murder?"

"Not one hundred per cent of the time. Mrs. Zuckerman—*is* it Mrs., by the way?—"

"You ought to know, if anyone. Being so pally with her."

"Consulting her professionally, not personally pally. Anyway, Lorelei was, but the rest of us were in and out at least once."

"Let's get this straight. What exactly was the set-up? You were all four in her sitting-room, right?"

"That's it: Martti, Felicity, Lorelei and me."

"What were you doing?"

"Talking about markets, agents' percentages, current trends—and drinking."

"You were all participating?"

Wes thought.

"We were all drinking. I don't remember Martti contributing to the conversation. But he was there all right. Felicity chipped in with her contribution now and then, but mostly it was me and Lorelei. Kenya is pretty remote from writing circles, you see, and I'm trying to use every minute of this trip to wise myself up. As far as the commercial side of the romance business is concerned, Lorelei is the bee's knees."

"I think I get the picture. Now what about when you left the room—the three of you who did."

"I left twice: once very briefly, to go to the loo. The other time I went to get some copies of my books. They're published by a firm in Cape Town, though I've also sold one or two to an American publisher. We were talking about production standards, and I wanted to get Lorelei's opinion on the sort of job the South African people did."

"How long did this take?"

"The Norskies asked me that, of course. At most ten minutes. They weren't in the drawer, as I thought. I found I hadn't unpacked them, so I had to get my suitcase down from on top of the wardrobe. Probably about five minutes, but at most ten."

"And the other three were there when you left, and there when you came back?"

"Yes, they were."

"You can't know that they didn't leave the room while you were away."

"That's true . . . But Felicity had just got drinks . . . you're not suggesting Lorelei nipped out, down to the boathouse, drowned Amanda and nipped back—all while I was away?"

"I'm just keeping possibilities in mind."

"Remember that she wouldn't expect me to be away so long. And even if her illness is a fake —which I *don't* believe—she is still a woman of —what?—sixty-five? Rather more, I'd have guessed. If you can see it, I must say I can't."

"And Felicity Maxwell?"

"She went to the bar to get fill-ups when necessary."

"How long did that take her, roughly?"

"I didn't notice. I was deep in conversation. You'd better ask her yourself."

"And the Finn?"

"Twice or three times to the loo. My impression—it's only that—is that these were fairly short visits. He came back, or wavered his way back, to his glass."

"Right. That seems fairly satisfactory. And you were all four in the room until the body was found?"

"That's right. As far as I was concerned, it was a really useful session. But the party was in fact just breaking up when we heard . . . well, when we heard your sister doing her nut. Very understandably, of course."

We had come to a stop near the path that led down to the boathouse. We turned for a moment and looked back to the house. Figures disappeared from the windows: I was still the observed of observers. I said:

"I must confess, a male writer of romances who is a white man from Kenya still strikes me as an oddity. No—sorry, I didn't mean to say anything rude: it strikes me as in need of some explanation. It's something so unusual that it makes me curious. Would you mind telling me something about yourself?"

Wes Mackay said slowly:

"No . . . I suppose I *am* a bit of an oddity, though I've never thought of it like that . . . I should say that I'm not a member of the filthy-rich, gin-slinging and wife-swapping Kenyan aristocracy that you're always reading about these days—the people who created such glorious scandals and juicy murders back in the 'thirties. If it wasn't for Independence I'd hardly be on speaking terms with that lot, let alone visiting terms. But as it is they've decreed that all whites should stick together, so all the barriers are broken down (which doesn't mean we're unconscious of them), and I get to put my toe over the stately thresholds now and again."

"What did your family do, if they didn't sling gin?"

"My grandfather owned a general store in Bura. My father was a younger son, and he organized safaris, acted as local rep for British and American travel firms. We're Scottish, very provincial, and in my grandfather's case, very narrow-minded. Like most of the whites in Kenya, we've weathered Independence without too many problems. We're not on any gravy-train any longer, but we jog along pretty comfortably."

"And you? What did you do before you took up . . . writing?"

"Oh, all sorts. Took tourists up in two-seater planes. Worked on a game reserve, and in the hotel business. But you're not really asking about that, are you? You're curious how I came to take up writing mush."

"I suppose it was a roundabout way of getting on to that."

"It's quite simple, though I suppose a bit unusual. I should tell you that I've always been a bit of . . . well, what used to be known as a ladies' man. More than a bit, actually. Which is one way I do fit into the Kenyan settler tradition. Women have always been at the centre of my life, one way or another. Every sort of affair, from one night stands upwards. But I've only ever loved once or twice . . . maybe three times . . . And the big love of my life, the woman I lived with for nearly five years, died . . . of leukemia. I don't want to talk about it, but I used to visit her in hospital, for months, until the end. You know what it's like if you go in the afternoon and evening, month after month. When you've asked what they had for lunch, and talked about the temperature outside, there's not much to say, however much you love them . . . And I had to go in . . . I had to see her . . . Before long, when she was in too much pain to hold a book, I started to read to her, the sort of books she loved. You can sneer, but I didn't."

"I'm not sneering. So you got to know the product?"

"That's right. Well, books aren't always easy to get hold of in Africa. The merest hint of an exchange crisis and the supply tends to dry up. And Lilian always remembered, always knew if she'd read something before, which was surprising, when they're all so similar. There came a time, three or four months before the end, when I realized that we were going to run out . . . And when I got home from the hospital that night, I sat down to write one. I did it in three evenings, on small paper I could slip inside a paperback. She never noticed . . . liked it . . . so I wrote another, and another, and I was reading one of mine to her when she died. That's the whole story."

"I see. So you even found you preferred it to taking tourists on safari, and suchlike?"

Wes Mackay shrugged.

"I don't know. Safari—yes; tourists—no. The sort who want to go pretend big-game hunting are really . . . But the point was that most of the jobs we whites had been doing in Kenya for fifty or sixty years were being taken over by the blacks—naturally enough, but it didn't make it any less bitter. They definitely don't want whites in a lot of jobs because it hurts national pride. Now here was a job where I would be independent of government, independent of corruption, political change, and independent of any sort of boss except the Great Reading Public. And if I had to leave the country, I could go to any-bloody-where on the globe and still have the same career. That was the crucial factor, because life is pretty uncertain anywhere in Africa these days. And it's turned out very satisfactorily. It's turned out great, in fact."

"I see. Yes, that does make it easier to understand. Tell me, what kind of contact have you had with other romantic writers, before you came here?"

"None."

"Never been on this sort of jamboree before?"

"No way. This is the big treat of my writing life so far. This sort of jaunt costs money, you know."

"So you knew no one here before you arrived?"

"I tell you, these people were just names to me. When I got the delegates' list I went along to the library and looked them up in *Twentieth-Century Romantic Novelists*. It may seem incredible to you, but this is my job, and so far I've been doing it thousands of miles from anyone who's doing the same thing. Soon I'll go *back* to being thousands of miles from anyone doing the same thing. I want gen, tips, I want to know about trends in the market, I want *contacts*."

"Fair enough," I said. "I'd better get this thing sorted out, or you'll be chafing at the bit at all the wasted time."

"Oh, I wouldn't mind if we could just be allowed to go walking in the mountains a bit," Wes said, as we walked back towards the house. "And there are one or two people here who still have plenty to give me." He added, without looking at me: "That Maryloo Parker seems to know a thing or two."

"Yes," I said. "You've hit the nail on the head there. If I were you I'd get on to Maryloo Parker."

We parted in the lounge, and I mounted the stairs towards Lorelei Zuckerman's rooms. It seemed as well to get this quadruple alibi sorted out as early as possible. However, when I knocked on the door of the suite's sitting-room, Felicity Maxwell opened the door and slipped out into the corridor.

"Mrs. Zuckerman is in the middle of her afternoon rest. She always sleeps around this time."

"Ah," I said. "I wanted to talk to her about last night. But of course I wouldn't want you to disturb her."

"The question doesn't arise," said Felicity. "I never disturb her."

She looked me straight in the eye, and I considered myself snubbed. She was a rather gauche, provincial creature, in her square-shouldered linen dress and the string of artificial beads, but there was a certain strength about her too—both moral and physical. She had something of my sister Cristobel's obstinacy, though I guessed there was a sharper brain behind it.

"Perhaps we two could talk, then," I suggested. Felicity Maxwell considered.

"Very well. But I'd rather not use the sitting-room, in case we wake her. Perhaps you would come along to my room?"

We walked down the corridor past Lorelei's bedroom, and went into Felicity's, which was next door. No doubt this was so that Lorelei could bang on the wall for her if she needed her, or merely if she felt like it. I could just picture her doing it. Felicity's bedroom was spartan but functional, like the rest, but it was cluttered with more luggage than most, which I guessed was mostly Mrs. Zuckerman's. Felicity gestured me to a hard upright chair, and herself sat on the bed.

"Right. Can we be fairly quick? She will probably wake up in twenty minutes or so."

"Of course. I'm interested for the moment in last night in Mrs. Zuckerman's room. What can you tell me about it?"

She replied without hesitation.

"I saw you talking outside to Mr. Mackay. I doubt if I can add anything. He and Mrs. Zuckerman talked about professional matters—me too, when I had anything to say. The Swede—is he a Swede?"

"Finn."

"Right. The Finn sat there, pretty comatose,

but drinking steadily. You'll be wanting to know about alibis, I suppose?"

"Certainly."

"Lorelei was in the sitting-room the whole time, of course. The Finn went to the john—twice I think. Mr. Mackay went to the john once, and once went to get some books. I fetched fresh drinks from the bar when necessary."

"How long were those various absences?"

"I didn't particularly notice. The visits to the john lasted I suppose as long as visits to the john do last—know what I mean?"

I nodded. I too visited the john.

"Though I suppose with the Finn I was a bit more aware than I otherwise would be—wondering whether he would make it there, and make it back. I would think he probably took rather longer than usual, but I couldn't be sure. Mackay was pretty much what one would expect."

"And his excursion to his room?"

"Longer . . . Of course I didn't time it."

"What were you doing while he was away?"

"Doing?"

"Well, there you were, Mrs. Zuckerman and the comatose Finn. Most of the conversation up to that point had been between Mrs. Zuckerman and Mackay. What happened when he left? Did you make conversation with the Finn?"

"Oh no. I don't think that would have been possible. He hardly said a word all evening . . . I remember I plumped Mrs. Zuckerman up in her chair, poured her a brandy . . . got her a couple of the digestive biscuits that she likes to nibble. Maybe we talked a bit—about whether she was tired, that sort of thing. He wasn't away that long."

"A quarter of an hour?"

She frowned.

"I wouldn't have thought so . . . But then time means less when . . . when you've had a couple of drinks."

"Well, let's get on to the drinks. It was you who fetched them from the bar?"

"That's right."

"How often?"

She thought.

"Three times is what I told the Norwegian police, and I think that's right. The third time it was just a refill for the Finn."

"Otherwise you were getting drinks for all four?"

"Three. Mrs. Zuckerman has her own brandy."

"Was there any delay at the bar? How long would each trip have taken you?"

"I don't remember any particular difficulty. People seemed to be spinning their drinks out, so there was no queue. Of course, I didn't time myself, but I would have said not more than ten minutes."

"Do you remember when these trips were?"

"Oh no . . . Wait . . . The second time I went there was a little portable television switched on behind the bar. The lady who runs the place wanted to watch because it was Thursday, and there was a P. D. James serial on television. We looked at the clock, and it was nearly nine. You were there in the bar, I remember."

"That's right, I would have been."

"And the last time I went must have been half an hour or so after that. The rest of us hadn't finished our drinks, not by a long chalk, but the Finn seemed to want more. It would have been a quarter of an hour or twenty minutes after I got back to the suite that we heard your sister—"

"Having hysterics. Well, thank you. That was very clear and helpful."

"The times are approximate only."

"Now, had either you or Mrs. Zuckerman met Amanda Fairchild before you came to this conference?"

"I'd rather you let Mrs. Zuckerman answer for herself, in general, but in this case I can say pretty definitely 'no,' for both of us."

"What about the other delegates?"

"I had met none of them before. Mrs. Zuckerman does not fraternize widely, so this has meant I haven't had a great deal of contact with any other writers. Mrs. Zuckerman will no doubt be able to tell you which of them she has met before."

"You say 'Mrs. Zuckerman.' She has been married, then?"

"I believe so." I waited for more, but after a pause she said: "I would much rather you asked Mrs. Zuckerman any questions pertaining to herself. You must realize that anything I might tell you would be mere hearsay."

"Of course. Still, you can testify that there is no husband in evidence at the moment."

"That is correct."

"Perhaps you wouldn't mind telling me how you became Mrs. Zuckerman's—what?—secretary? nurse?"

"Nurse-companion. Naturally she has a secretary in New York. No, I don't mind at all. My mother and I lived in the next apartment to hers. My mother was an invalid for several years before she died, and I was always with her. After her death Mrs. Zuckerman offered me my present position, which I was happy to accept."

"Why?"

The brutality of my question seemed to startle her.

"I beg your pardon?"

"Why were you happy to accept? Having nursed one invalid, most people wouldn't want to go straight over to nursing another. Mrs. Zuckerman seems not to enjoy good health."

"Lorelei has a heart condition, which is likely to prove fatal within eighteen months or so. Some people have a gift for nursing, Superintendent. With some it's children, others it's old people. I must say I've never found it a wearisome chore. But I'm not going to pretend I'm being entirely unselfish either."

"Oh? You hope for something in Mrs. Zuckerman's will?"

She pursed up her mouth, and looked very Sunday School indeed.

"Come, come, Mr. Trethowan. Of course not. Nothing of the sort. Why, I wouldn't even be able to claim to be a servant of particularly long standing."

"I'm sorry. That was a crude, policeman's conjecture."

"What I meant was that I, in my small way, am also a romantic writer. Three books to date, but I am learning my craft slowly. I could hardly learn it in better circumstances than by being with Mrs. Zuckerman. I act as a sort of sounding-board while her books take shape, and all the time I'm learning more and more about the art of romance writing—and of course the commercial side of it."

"Quite."

"Mrs. Zuckerman is very generous with advice and information on the commercial level, as Mr. Mackay will testify. Many people wouldn't expect it, but she is."

"You like her?"

She looked at me with a rather aggravatingly upright air.

"Affection doesn't enter into it. Lorelei wouldn't want or expect it to. I feel enormous gratitude and respect, and that is enough for her."

"And she is, I imagine, enormously rich?"

"You keep coming back to money, I don't know why. I repeat, that is the sort of thing you ought to talk to her about."

"But you do know that she sells well."

"Oh, certainly. Her sales figures are stupendous. I can see you despise romance writing, Superintendent." I made a gesture of dissent which was clearly as unconvincing as it was insincere. "You think of it as dream fodder for women. You can equally say that Westerns and war books are dream fodder for men, but I don't imagine you despise them half as much. All popular literature ministers to pretty basic human impulses; otherwise it wouldn't be popular literature. And if you do it skilfully—and Lorelei is supremely skilful—I don't see why you should be ashamed. She certainly isn't, and I don't feel ashamed for her."

I felt rebuked. Felicity Maxwell followed up her advantage by getting up.

"She'll be waking up soon. I think I've told you all I can." She led the way out into the corridor, and shut the door in a firm, housekeeperly sort of way, as if she suspected I might want to nip back in. "If you wait for a little, I'll get her into the sitting-room and make her presentable."

She went into Mrs. Zuckerman's bedroom, leaving me casting around in my mind for images that could represent Lorelei before she had been made to look presentable.

11

Come into My Parlour

Mrs. Zuckerman having been made presentable, I was summoned into the presence, to find her sitting in an armchair with the sources of her comfort around her—a bottle, a packet of cigarettes, a plateful of digestive biscuits. The chair she was in was probably a perfectly good chair under any normal bum, but she managed to make it look uncomfortable. It was the cheerless expression, the straight back, the black bombazine dress above the thick black stockings, the air of a lifestyle deliberately chosen to exclude joy. Or to exclude what normal people would call joy, for there was about her generally some substratum of self-satisfaction, a hugging of herself over some experience or some power, which I found disgusting but which was indicative of some twisted form of pleasure. I didn't necessarily connect it, though, with the death of Amanda Fairchild. I had felt it in her since she arrived.

When Felicity Maxwell introduced me, Lore-

lei Zuckerman gazed on me malevolently, and
gave me not so much as a nod. This was clearly
one of her little routines, for I remembered her
practising it on Amanda on our first night. Her
mouth was working, as if she was masticating
some choice titbit, but beyond that she registered no reaction to me. She said: "Put another
cushion at my back," and the eyes glinted when
Felicity hurried to obey. She got more pleasure,
I think, from ordering about this cool, self-pos-
sessed girl than she would from tyrannizing
over a drudge. Being slave-master to born slaves
is the first pleasure that palls in the power game.
Lorelei's tastes were now much more recondite.

When Felicity had sat me down, she said in
her competent-nurse voice: "Well, I'll be in my
room, should you want me, Lorelei." And then
she went out.

The brandy and water at Lorelei's elbow had
been mixed to her specifications before I had
been let in. Now, still registering nothing at my
presence in the room, Mrs. Zuckerman took a
sip, and looked ahead of her thoughtfully, as if
meditating some particularly luckless star-cross-
ing of her fictional lovers.

"I suppose you can guess that I would like to
discuss last night, Mrs. Zuckerman," I began,
trying to speak in a casual voice to demonstrate
that I was not impressed by her performance.
Her strong, square, bombazined shoulders
sketched a shrug.

"I don't see why," she said in her harsh drawl,
like a badly-played clarinet. "There were three
people to testify that I was here all evening."

She thought for a moment, and then added: "Two of whom had all their wits about them."

She had anticipated my next point, no doubt intentionally.

"Exactly," I said. "One was, if I'm not mistaken, thoroughly soused. And if one of the other two was out of the room, and if the other of them was in your pay or your confidence . . ."

Lorelei laughed harshly.

"If you think I'm a sham cripple, you can get all the medical details from my doctor, my heart specialist and my hospital. Maxwell will give you all the details."

"I don't seriously doubt your medical condition," I said, though I did make a note in my mind to get the details from Felicity. "But everything has to be checked. And it's important I talk to you to establish the alibis of the other three. Your corroboration is vital."

Mrs. Zuckerman's face assumed a contemptuous expression. An alibi from her, it seemed, was to be regarded as a favour rather than as a right. She volunteered nothing. I said:

"Your nurse-companion fetched fresh drinks for herself and the two men. Do you remember when and how often she did that?"

Felicity Maxwell had left Lorelei's cigarettes and matches on a little table by the left arm of Lorelei's chair. Now, slowly, she took a cigarette, fitted it into a long holder, lit it, and puffed smoke in my direction. It was a piece of insolence, or perhaps a display of power and prerogative. I sat there, neither helping nor reacting.

She was all too used to having people jump to her whims. Finally she spoke, in that harsh, un-ingratiating drawl:

"She certainly renewed the drinks. More than once. I would guess three times. But I had my own drink. I drink nothing but brandy and water. Except for an occasional sherry. I certainly didn't notice what time she fetched them. Why should I?"

"No reason at all. And the men, too, left the room on various errands, did they not? What about the Finn, for example?"

She went through the same process of lengthy consideration—making it seem as though she was considering not what to tell me, but whether.

"I think he went to the john. If he didn't, he must have a pretty peculiar constitution. Don't remember anything about it, only that he went."

"And Mr. Mackay?"

Again that aggravating silence. Thank God we were not being broadcast.

"Is that his name? He went to fetch some books. His own, of course. Don't remember anything more about it."

"Do you remember how long these various absences were?"

"No."

"Miss Maxwell's absences, for example, would have been longer than the Finn's?"

"I imagine so. It would take longer to go to the bar and back than to go to the john."

"But you don't *remember* that it was longer?"

"I've told you, no."

"Or Mr. Mackay's trip to his room?"

"He took a long time. A lot longer than his damned little books deserved. But Maxwell was plumping up my cushions and passing me a drink. I don't remember *how* long."

I gave up that line of questioning.

"Tell me, when did you first meet Amanda Fairchild?"

She registered the change of direction by putting a particularly disagreeable expression on her face and blowing smoke straight into my face.

"I first *met* (as you put it) Fairchild when she forced herself upon me during my first dinner in this place. You all watched. You will remember."

"I do indeed. So you had never met at previous conferences, or publishers' parties?"

"I've told you when we first met. I do not repeat information."

I sucked in my lips and gazed at her sourly. She gazed at me sourly back. This interview was beginning to have its comic sides. I chanced my arm, opting to give rather than request information. I only hoped it was correct.

"You lived for a time in London, Mrs. Zuckerman."

"Who told you that?"

For once the come-back was immediate.

"That doesn't matter. When was this?"

"I don't know." She shrugged. "Some time in the 'sixties. 'The swinging 'sixties!' Ha! London didn't swing for me."

"What were you doing there?"

She went back to the long pause, sucking her gums.

"I was married. To an Englishman. For a time."

"The marriage broke down?"

The smile, that I had seen before submerged in her face, for once broke out. It was the most unlovely smile I had ever seen.

"The man did. He was a wimp. Husbands always are, I suspect."

"You've been married often?"

"Once. Just to say I'd tried it."

"You stayed on in Britain for a while, did you?"

Pause.

"For a while."

"What did you do for a living?"

"I had alimony payments. I . . . wrote."

"Ah. You wrote romantic love stories?"

"I wrote many kinds of fiction. Romance among them."

"Were you published by the Tamworth group?"

Pause.

"I don't recall that name . . . My agent long ago bought up my early titles . . . I wouldn't have had anything to do with my early publishers for years, and neither would he."

"But you would remember the pseudonyms the books were published under, would you not? You seem to have a gift for names. Were any of your books published under the name Amanda Fairchild?"

"Emphatically not."

"But you do use pseudonyms?"

"For different sorts of work I have different names. That's perfectly normal in this profession. But I always invent my own. I would not invent a name like Amanda Fairchild."

"Why not?"

That disagreeable smile crossed her face again, briefly.

"It is too . . . happy-sounding. Too innocent. I don't like gilding the lily. I prefer a name with a touch of mystery . . . or danger. As with le Neve. Definitely guilty, wouldn't you say?"

"It's not a case I've gone into—not a very interesting one from a policeman's point of view. What about your career before and after your stay in Great Britain?"

A smoke-ring was blown impertinently to surround my nose.

"What *about* my career before and after my stay in Great Britain?"

"Perhaps you would care to tell me what you've done and when?"

"I would not, particularly."

"I see. Is there any reason for your . . . reticence?"

"None. Except that I am a person who has always lived my life for myself, not for the benefit of other people. I was here, immobile, for what I gather was the whole of the vital period. I can't see any reason why you should need the facts of my career, such as they are."

"Put it down to idle curiosity."

"I am not interested in other people's idle curiosity."

"That's odd. Surely it's the basis of the fiction-reading habit. You should remember, Mrs. Zuckerman, that a policeman not only has a great deal of idle curiosity: he also has a great deal of power, when it comes to the gathering of information. I have no doubt that the major events of your life are set out in some computer data bank somewhere or other in your country or mine. I can get hold of the facts I need by contacting the FBI. What could you do about it? Do you have a host of powerful friends who would rush to intervene on your behalf?"

She stared stonily back. Then she said: "My publisher does what I tell him."

"It would be much better for you if you told me voluntarily what I want to know."

She stubbed out her cigarette, flicked a knob to eject the stub from the holder, and then—unusually for her—immediately put another one in and lit it. Finally, unemotionally, as if reciting facts entered upon a card, she said:

"I grew up in New York. My family were immigrants, German immigrants. *Not* Jewish . . . I went to the Juilliard School, sang a bit in opera. I joined the army in 1945. Served for nearly twenty years. I got out when I married this damned limey. His name was Poppleton—can you imagine? It was a relief to go back to my family name. But I stuck it for three years. Got tired of trying to give him some backbone. Started writing. War books, historicals, thrillers, romances. Found romance paid best. Stuck with it. Got darned sick of London. All the mess, and the strikes. Went back to New York. Lived there ever since."

It was like one of those entries in the one-volume edition of the *Dictionary of National Biography*. It told you everything and nothing. I took up, for convenience, her last point.

"Alone? Have you lived alone, until Miss Maxwell became your companion?"

"I have. Since I separated from my husband."

"Have you had much contact with your fellow writers?"

"None. Practically none."

"Nor done any of the promotional things that publishers like authors to do—lecture tours, signing sessions, television appearances, that sort of thing?"

"I once did a signing session at one of the big bookstores in New York." She gazed viciously at me, freezing any potential laughter. "My publisher did not think that it helped sales."

"I see . . . So you were not closely acquainted with any of the American or English writers at the conference?"

"No."

"Not acquainted at all, in fact?"

"No."

"Why did you decide to come to this conference?"

I dropped that one swiftly, and she took her time about answering, taking a long, vicious pull on her cigarette.

"I am an old woman. I have only a short time to live, so I'm told. I've sat alone in my flat, writing, for years on end. When I was young, in the army, I travelled . . . travelled all the time. Consumed new experiences . . . It's what I've used in my writing . . . I thought I should do it once more, now I have a companion." A dim, mean sparkle suddenly illumined her eye. "My publisher paid for the trip."

"I see."

I felt like asking her if she'd been having a wow of a time up to now, but I refrained. I sat there thinking, but came up with very little that could lead to further questions.

"How often did you speak to Amanda Fairchild in the three days you were here together?" I asked her at last.

"Once."

"The occasion you mentioned, at dinner on the first evening?"

She inclined her head.

"You've had no further indirect dealings with her?"

"None."

"What was your opinion of her?"

"A fool." That came out like a whiplash. If she'd wanted to she could not have stopped it, and she gave no sign that she regretted it. She went on, smiling that unpleasant smile: "You can write foolish books for foolish people without *being* a fool. She was one."

But there, I thought, Lorelei showed that she was one of the ones who had been fooled.

Once out of Lorelei's sitting-room, I walked along the corridor to the little bedroom that had the direct telephone line out. Behind me I heard a door open and shut, and then another: Felicity Maxwell going straight in to Lorelei's suite. Once in the room I sat in the drab little desk chair and tried to do some hard thinking. *All* these people, and not just Lorelei, were so far from their home environments, so far from any easy checking and cross-checking of their statements. However little they told me—and Lorelei's account of herself could hardly have been more skeletal—I had either to take it on trust or go back to their home base to get it confirmed.

I didn't mistrust the Norwegian police, but I did like working with my own people. I got on the 'phone to Inspector Joplin at the Yard, and asked him to get on to the FBI. The information I asked for was not just on Lorelei Zuckerman, but on Felicity Maxwell, Maryloo Parker and Patti Drewe. The whole American gang. Then, for the benefit of the Yard computer, I gave the names of the British gang as well. That more or less sewed it up, except for rogue elephants like Kenyans and Finns. And Norwegians. I remem bered that I hadn't wised Stein and Svein up on Miss Ragnhild Sørby. Maybe I should, I thought.

12
Cold Facts

❦

Before I left that useful little room, with the telephone line that bypassed the guest-house switchboard, I rang Jan in Oppheim. I had had a message sent up to her that morning, but as she told me, that had been quite unnecessary.

"Everyone was talking about it at breakfast," she said. "It had been on the radio news at half past seven. Apparently they have hardly any murders in Norway, apart from the occasional drunks who bash each other into oblivion, so there was a great twitter about it, and someone explained to me what they were going on about —very privately, so Daniel couldn't hear, as if it were one of the facts of life. I explained this was one of the facts of life he knows quite a bit about. The Norwegians say they haven't been so excited about anything since the Swedish Prime Minister was assassinated. Oh dear: I *didn't* mean to be flippant about it. I didn't, funnily enough, dislike her."

"Nor did I—at least, not most of the time."

"I realized as soon as I heard that you would get roped in. Tell me the details."

I gave her the barest possible account of the finding of Amanda's body. I usually did it when I was at home, so I was damned if I would be bound by any Norwegian police rules. Jan seized at once on the most picturesque detail.

"A bough of cherry blossom? But that must be terribly significant."

"Or else supremely and deliberately irrelevant," I countered churlishly.

"Well, yes—I can see that. Still, it does give one furiously to think, doesn't it? Leaving aside Lorelei, as the most obvious, and physically incapable anyway, who is it most likely to be? Granted the cherry blossom, I would plump for a Jealous Rival."

"I thought you were discarding the obvious."

"Oh, but a jealous rival does rather fit in with the whole *mise-en-scène*, doesn't it? Every romance has to have one. Even Jane Eyre has her Blanche Ingram."

Jan knows a lot about the Brontës, though her acquaintance with most of the rest of the English classics comes from BBC television serials. Thus, she pretends to know *Bleak House*, but she knows nothing of Mrs. Jellyby.

"Which of the assembled competitors would you promote to Jealous Rival?" I asked, humouring her.

"Let me see . . . I think I'd plump for Arthur Biggs. I can imagine his innards being ge-nawed by an ingrowing jealousy, can't you?"

"Indeed I can. However, there is one fatal drawback to your scenario."

"What's that?"

"Amanda didn't write a single one of the books published under her name."

"What?"

"She was merely a front figure, nothing more."

"How many of the delegates knew that?"

"I don't know, though it may be necessary to find out. However, the one person who most certainly did know was, is, Arthur Biggs."

"Hmmm. Get back to me, Perry, when I've had time to think this over. I need to chew on it."

"Well, don't let it ge-naw at your innards. Love to Daniel."

So that was Jan given something to do, as she wandered through the hills that were alive with the sound of music. I hoped she came up with something better than I had managed so far. It was time for me now to bring myself up to date on whatever Forensic had come up with, but first what I really needed was something to eat. I had had nothing since breakfast, and my stomach was reminding me that for the last few days I had eaten regularly and often, and that it had liked the fact. I wandered downstairs, and saw that practically the whole cast of suspects were seated around tables on the porch, over teapots and plates. The exceptions were, apart from the Zuckerman party, Cristobel and Bernard, who were probably holding hands on a rock somewhere in the grounds. I wandered to join the tea-party, and found that I was very much more welcome than I had been at breakfast. Which was just as well, because the eats consisted mainly of biscuits, and I ate most of them. They, after all, had doubtless had lunch, and anyway the biscuits were rather dreary. They sat around at their little tables, like actors on a stage set, and watched me closely.

"I suppose it's not the slightest use asking you how things are going?" began Mary Sweeny. Many of the others looked at her with irritation. They had obviously been hoping to approach the topic with more subtlety.

"Not the slightest," I agreed equably. "Quite apart from the fact that I haven't spoken to the police since this morning, so I don't know much more than you do."

"We gather her publisher's here," said Maryloo Parker, "and that you've spoken to him."

I nodded and said nothing.

"Or *rather*," Patti Drewe put in, "one should perhaps say the man who created the Amanda Fairchild persona. Created it on the bodies of nameless and doubtless underpaid scribblers."

I shot Arthur Biggs a glance of distaste. There was not now going to be any chance of launching that particular line of questioning on anybody with any hope of surprising them.

"Did you want me to keep it quiet?" he asked airily. I ignored him and ate another biscuit.

"Do there happen to be any of the nameless and exploited scribes here present?" I asked casually, sitting down at the only empty table and gazing out over the lawn as if I hoped to see a squirrel. When I looked back everybody shook their heads.

"It came on all of us as a terrific surprise," said Mary Sweeny. "Obviously if anyone had written any of those titles, they would have *known*."

"Quite," I said. "Though surprise is an extremely easy emotion to counterfeit." I swung my chair backwards and looked around at them in a somewhat lordly fashion, rather as my late great-grandfather must have surveyed deputations of foundry-hands. "And the surprise, surely, can't have been *entirely* universal. You, Mrs. Biggs, must have known—and surely you, too, Mr. Manning. Wasn't it one of the things that you three . . . chewed over together?"

"Oddly enough, it wasn't," said Manning, and Mrs. Biggs murmured: "No, indeed."

"Funny," I commented.

"Amanda Fairchild wasn't a very interesting figure, looked at from the point of view of the art of romance," elaborated Everard Manning, with the air of a 'thirties Oxford don, very much *manqué*. "A backward-looking figure in almost every way. She certainly cannot be said to have changed the possibilities of the romance form."

"Ah," I said.

"What we're all rather worried about—" put in Mary Sweeny.

"Well, not *worried*," said Arthur Biggs.

"—worried about, is this question of what we were all doing at the relevant time."

"That's always rather difficult," I said. "Particularly if there was any sort of party or gathering."

"Well, you know, Perry, that we were all in the bar," said Maryloo, giving me a vanity-of-human-wishes sort of look. "But you know too that one is never in the bar *all the time*."

"Oh, quite," I said.

"I mean, some of us went to our rooms, I imagine, some of us took a stroll, and nearly all of us went to the lavatory," said Mary Sweeny.

"Naturally," put in Arthur Biggs pompously. His manner always grated on me, so I got stroppy.

"Oh, I don't know about that."

"What on earth do you mean?" asked Wes Mackay.

I stirred in my seat, sated with biscuit, and stood up.

"I'm not sure that it was natural that you all, apparently, went to the lavatory."

"For God's sake, what could be more natural than a call of nature?" demanded Maryloo.

"One makes calls of nature when one has been drinking," I said, preparing to go back to the house. "So far as I've observed since I came here, the price of drinks in Norway has prevented most people from drinking anything much at all."

I exited on this line, and had a quiet internal chuckle over the frame of mind in which it left them as I walked through the lounge. Like most such smart-alec remarks, it didn't bear too great a weight being laid on it: there was water on the table at dinner, and no doubt some of the men had been drinking beer; again, women often go to the lavatory to repair their make-up, or to see to various little intimate matters. Still, there was at least *something* in it. The water at table had not, as a rule, been drunk in any great quantity: I had noticed this because it was wonderful water, such as British water may once have been, but had not been in many a long year—pure, delectable rainwater. Patti Drewe drank an awful lot of water with her meal, as many Americans do, but nobody else much had done so. Maryloo, I remembered, had shared a half-bottle of Jugoslav Riesling with Felicity Maxwell. None of the British writers had drunk much water, and the Arthur Biggs table had shared another half-bottle of wine. So it was just about worth considering, though one always had to remember that bladders were funny things. And it was quite possible that writing romances led to what one of my Australian relatives calls a "frequency."

All was quiet upstairs in the corridor. Even the Finn's room, outside which the brawny sergeant sat reading a Mickey Mouse comic, was silent as the grave. I found Stein and Svein in Amanda's room, confabbing in their quiet-voiced way over the results from the police labs in Bergen. They welcomed me with genuine friendliness, pulled up a chair for me, and poured me a beaker of coffee from the percolator which stood on its little warmer in the corner —no doubt provided by the proprietress in recognition of a chronic Norwegian need. Then we all three got down to discussing the developments of the day.

"First of all, she was deliberately drowned," said Stein. "There was a vicious karate blow to the neck, but that wasn't what killed her. No doubt it sent her toppling into the water, but there are bruises on the shoulder which show that she was held under. It would have taken perhaps three or four minutes."

"Right," I said. "After which the cherry blossom bough was thrown in on top of her."

"That's right," agreed Stein. "Though by the way, she was never entirely in the water. One foot and calf were still almost dry—they must have remained on the landing-stage. But your point, I take it, is: why not push the body out into the fjord and make *some* attempt to suggest that this was a natural drowning?"

"Yes. This proclaimed itself as murder."

"Yes. We're puzzled by that too. Now, those bits of paper that you picked out of the water—very sensibly. Just one is vital—the rest is supermarket bills, old envelopes and so on. One is a little piece of paper—*Kvalevåg Gjestgiveri* notepaper."

"Ah. There's plenty in the lounge, and a few bits in each room."

"Exactly. Anyone could get hold of it. And the message is typewritten—but unfortunately on the typewriter in the little office off the lounge."

"The proprietress's?"

"That's right. There's no money kept there, and it's always open. In fact, I gather she's said that one or two of the guests asked if it was all right to use it, and she told them it was perfectly OK."

"Damn. Does she remember who?"

"Yes—Maryloo Parker and Mrs. Biggs."

"*Mrs.* Biggs?"

"Yes—apparently she types her husband's works, and all his correspondence. But Fru Tønnesen—that's the lady who owns this place—says that others took this as a general permission."

"Double damn. And what did the thing say?"

"It just read: '9:30. OK?' "

"Short and to the point. But apparently not so *much* so that Amanda felt any suspicion. You're not going to get anything very conclusive about finger pressure out of *that*. Is there anything else?"

Stein stirred in his chair, and his rather bland face furrowed at the forehead.

"A couple of things, both of them rather odd. Or unexpected, perhaps I should say. First there were all these Roberts that we had to check, to see if they might have been the man, the boyfriend, she was writing to."

"Yes?"

"Well, all of them deny any knowledge of her, outside her books, and all of them deny having met her. I must say that, without *really* being able to check up, because that would mean going minutely into all their life histories, *and* the victim's, still, I found most of their denials convincing. But the odd thing is that there is one of them who admits to having *seen* her."

"Seen her?"

"On scene—on *stage*."

I thought for a moment, to discover what was puzzling him.

"I suppose that is a little odd, since it wasn't much of a theatrical career."

"But the odd thing is that it was the Nigerian who had seen her—Robert Achinowuba. He said he saw her real name in *Happy Tears*, just as you did. He saw her as Celia in a British Council African tour of *As You Like It* in Nairobi in the early 'sixties."

"How strange. And you're quite sure that was *all*?"

"So he swears. And since apparently he was only sixteen at the time, it seems likely he's telling the truth. She may have had some sort of agent that we can check dates with. As it is, the age he says he was is borne out by his passport. He said he was taken from school—it was one of the big events of his young life, and he still has the programme at home. It was his only experience of Western drama before he began coming to Europe, which was fifteen or more years later. So that's one odd little coincidence."

"Right. We'll have to make of that what we can. What's—"

But I was interrupted by a sound that shattered the somewhat murky silence of the upper corridor—a voice raised in some doleful student ditty, such as was doubtless sung in the student residences of Helsinki, as they handed the twenty-fifth bottle around. We darted out into the corridor, and gazed disgustedly at the sergeant, who was looking at the Finn's door in dismay.

"May I make a suggestion?" I asked.

"Do," said Stein courteously.

"There must be some empty rooms some-where in the guest-house. There were several people arrived last night who were shunted off to the Kvalevåg Hotel. Put him in pyjamas, do a thorough body-search, and lock him in one of those. As it is, you won't be able to do much with him until the morning."

As Stein went off, melancholy and somewhat shamefaced, to see Mrs. Tønnesen and arrange it, I turned to Svein.

"As I was about to say, before I was so rudely interrupted—"

"You were going to ask about the other curi-ous thing."

"Yes."

"Well, perhaps it was not so curious. It just isn't quite what we expected, from what we'd heard of . . . Miss—I suppose it was Miss?—Fairchild."

"Amanda."

"Yes. Well, from an inspection of the bed-clothes, and from the pathologist's report—"

But I knew already what was coming.

"That doesn't seem right," I said.

"No. At some time in the fairly recent past, Amanda had—how do you put it nicely in En-glish?—engaged in sexual activity."

"Right. And judging by the letter to 'Robbie,' it wasn't with him."

"That's what we thought. Is this something you would have expected?"

"No," I said. "It's not something I would have expected at all."

13

Ladies' Man

It wasn't strictly part of my side of the inquiry, but when Stein and Svein said they were going to go and talk to Mrs. Tønnesen and the odd job boy, I decided to go along with them. The boy, at least, was important, because his position at the head of the lane leading to the guest-house could make him a prime witness. He it was who could set limits, if we believed him, to the list of suspects we needed to keep in mind.

Mrs. Tønnesen led us to a quiet corner of the kitchen, away from the muscular cook and her assistants. We sat round a table with a red checked cloth, feeling very much *au paysan*. The boy played with a knife, but he seemed nervous mainly because his English was to be on show and might be found wanting. Fru Tønnesen was careful in her English, but precise and perfectly collected.

The boy was called Gorm, poor soul, and he was the son of one of Fru Tønnesen's cousins. He had worked at Kvalevåg for the last two summers, thus earning much-needed cash (for I gathered from him that Norwegian students do not get grants, which doesn't say much for their much-boasted womb-to-tomb social security). Gorm had gone down to the bus stop at around a quarter to eight. The bus was due about eight, but it was a long time before he realized that this was not just a normal delayed arrival. He had stood there from about ten to eight until the bus arrived about ten twenty-five. If he had known about the accident and the blocked road he would have taken something to read, or his transistor. As it was, he had nothing to do but mooch around and look up and down the road.

He was adamant that no one had come down the road to the guest-house, nor had anyone left the guest-house to walk the road to Kvalevåg. Only my sister and Bernard had been down, to talk to him for a while. Even the locals had stayed away from the bar that evening, as they tended to when the long evenings came and the foreign tourists began to arrive. He was almost certain that no one had scuttled across the overgrown field that separated the guest-house from the road. To do that without his seeing them, they would have had to have left the road round the corner, tracked through a coppice, then propelled themselves practically on their belly through the long grass until they got to the trees around the guest-house lawn. He just didn't think it could be done without his noticing. Certainly he convinced all of us that it was highly unlikely.

"You must have been one of the last people to

see the lady alive," said Stein, speaking in his soft, unemotional voice. The boy screwed up his face and nodded, tapping nervously with his knife on the red-patterned cloth.

"How much did you have to do with her during her stay?"

He shrugged.

"I translated the article for her. Then on the night she died I translated her letter. Otherwise I just served her at table now and then, or in the bar."

"You weren't more friendly than that? You didn't do her more intimate services?"

When the boy understood what was being asked, he crimsoned, broke into Norwegian, and when he returned to English I understood him to say: "I'm young! I wouldn't think of it."

He seemed to be an ageist. His denials rang true. Amanda seemed like a mother-figure to him, though a less than comfortable one.

"Nevertheless," said Stein, turning to the proprietress, "these intimacies occurred with someone."

She pursed her lips.

"It happens."

"You have no idea with whom it happened in this case?"

"No. I make it my business not to know about the private affairs of my guests. The Norwegian tourist trade is mostly with older people, but they can on occasion . . . do most extraordinary things. You understand? It is better I not know. My bedroom is separate from the rest—I can get to it through the kitchen. If I am called, I go. Otherwise, it is none of my business."

"But you have seen her *with* the other guests? . . ."

"Of course. One sees, sometimes, the *beginnings* of things." (Was it my imagination, or did she look at me as she said that?) "But if one does not see the *end*, how does one know? With Mrs. —is it Mrs.?—Fairchild there was her *manner*. Very . . . free. Very . . . too friendly, like it was not always meant. How much do you read into that? Not much, very often. So I know nothing."

Stein sighed.

"Well, I suppose we'll have to leave it there." We got up. "I wish you could tell us how the Finn gets hold of his drink."

"He gets hold of it because he brought it with him."

"But we searched his room, and still he manages—"

"Did you look under the floorboards?"

"No. I never imagined—"

"You have no idea how cunning these drunks are. Not to mention all sorts of people you don't imagine to be drunks at all. If the idea that there had been a murder got through to him, then the idea that someone would want to dry him out— is that what you say?—probably got through to him too."

"Well, he won't find a private cellar under the floorboards in the new room."

"No," said Fru Tønnesen in her tight-lipped way, "that I can guarantee."

If the interview had done nothing else, it had firmly re-established the guilt of someone or other in the guest-house—somebody British, American, or indeed Norwegian. It did not escape my notice that the boy's insistence that nobody could have got past him to the guest-house also served to reinforce his own claim to have been at the roadside the whole of the relevant time. No doubt the police would check with motorists who passed at the time whether they noticed him. Certainly we couldn't entirely rule out, either, someone who had been hidden in the grounds from earlier in the evening, waiting for the nine-thirty assignation with Amanda, though the provenance of the notepaper made that unlikely. No, it was surely one of the guest-house people, with the overwhelming probability that it was one of the British or American guests.

"I wonder," I said, as we climbed the stairs to the lounge.

What I was remembering was the American publisher I had seen at the first day's opening gathering, and discussed with Maryloo Parker—the one, I mean, for whom books were synonymous with bedtime. I rather doubted whether he had slept with quite as many romantic authors as Maryloo Parker had implied—probably she suffered from a tendency to generalize out from her own experience—but still he could be a powerful source of gossip about the American writers, and perhaps even some of the British ones. What the hell was his name? I borrowed the list of delegates from Stein, who had it in his

folder, and flicked through it. Marriott Dulac—
that was it! Bloody silly name it was too, about as
convincing as Lorelei le Neve. Anyway, he was
staying at the Scandilux Hotel, which was con-
venient. I begged the car off Stein again, and
explained whom I wanted to see.

"You're not expecting to hear about the love-
life of Mrs. Zuckerman, I suppose?" asked Svein.

No, I said, I wasn't. I hadn't put any of my eggs
in that particular basket. Oddly enough, in the
event Lorelei was one of the people I got to hear
most about.

It was about six when I got back to the
Scandilux, and I was disappointed to be told that
Marriott Dulac was not in his room. I told the
girl on the desk I would check around. The bars
yielded up nothing except sipping romance
writers, but I found him finally in one of the
coffee lounges—inevitably with one of the writers. She was plain but pleasant-looking, and in
her thirties. Dulac was playing it pretty cool:
with someone more sexually and socially presti-
gious I could imagine him leaning forward in-
tensely, transfixing her with a display of his personality and of his interest in her. With this one
he sat back, swinging on the back legs of his
chair, toying with a piece of oozy chocolate cake
on his plate, and making it clear that he would
have her if he wanted her, and would be doing
her a favour to boot.

He was a big man, with a lot of flesh distrib-
uted over big bones. His face was large and
fleshy too, with the traditional thick, wet lips
and hair that had hardly begun to thin, or else

was being unobtrusively boosted. It was the confidence, verging on brashness, with which he presented his body that spoke of the sexual athlete, the punisher of bedsprings. I could see why Maryloo (in spite of her cynicism) had been attracted to him: he looked like Ted Kennedy on a good day.

"Mr. Dulac?" He looked up without irritation. Seduction was all in a day's work, and he was used to being interrupted in the middle of it. "I'm from Scotland Yard, and I'm helping with the investigation into Amanda Fairchild's death. I wonder if—some time—I could have a word with you."

"Sure. Delighted. Flattered." He looked it, too. He took the hand of his companion in his two big paws and patted it, in a gesture I had seen sugar-daddies do on the screen but never expected to see outside the cinema. "Say, honey, can we take this up at dinner, maybe? I'll see you then—make a point of it."

His companion took herself off obediently, and with a tactful lack of fuss. Some men had all the luck. He now added, under his breath, and with a conspiratorial wink at me: "If nothing better offers."

He insisted on fetching me a coffee from the counter, and as there was nobody at any of the nearby tables I decided that this was as good a place as anywhere to talk to him. Marriott Dulac's voice was unexpectedly musical and low—a bedroom voice, presumably, but not an unpleasant one.

"As I say, I'm flattered—truly flattered that

you want to talk to me, but I'm not quite sure why that is. I've never, to my knowledge, published anything by Amanda Fairchild."

"No, that's not why. You were pointed out to me, on the first day of the conference, as someone who had a wide experience among romance writers."

"Right! You're right there!" His face glowed with a smile of self-delight that was almost artless. "An unparalleled acquaintance with the species. But again, not—I regret to say—with Amanda Fairchild. She was less well-known in the States than she was in Europe. That's true of most British writers, I guess. American readers prefer something they can relate to pretty directly. Anyway, I don't recall her having made any American visit, so I didn't have the chance to get . . . acquainted."

"No—your name certainly hasn't come up in connection with Amanda. I was thinking more of the American writers who are staying at the *Kvalevåg Gjestgiveri*. Maryloo Parker, for instance . . ."

"Now there's a lady!" His face lit up. "Gamesome I'd call her. Ready for anything."

"Do you know anything about her background?"

"A little. I guess we've talked a fair bit while we've been together. And we have happened to coincide at a fair number of . . . congresses and things. She's a Midwesterner, good middle-class upbringing. Daddy was a banker or a solicitor—one of these solid professions, anyway—but something went badly wrong in Maryloo's late teens. I suspect a jail term for Daddy, but Maryloo is cagey. Anyway, it meant dropping out of college, doing a lot of grinding jobs—sales rep, beautician, canvassing—that sort of thing. She was married, briefly, to a teacher, and it was while she was married that she took up romance-writing. When the marriage collapsed she found she had a viable source of income, to supplement the alimony."

"What about on a personal level?"

"She's a sweet cookie. A clever chick. What more can I say?"

What more indeed? Character analysis in depth didn't seem to be his forte.

"Then there's Patti Drewe . . ."

He screwed up his face.

"Oh yeah, yeah. I don't know that I remember much . . . Sure we did—you know—but . . . Wait: she's got an invalid husband. You know, writing's a real last resort for folk in distress, financial, emotional, whatever. What would disgraced politicians do if they couldn't go away and write thrillers? Half my writers have problems getting their alimony, invalid husbands or by-blow children they want to put through college." (Rather rich that last point, I thought, coming from him.) "I seem to remember that Patti is a pretty good writer. Naturally I don't read many romances except those from our stable, but I think she's very competent. That's my impression of her: coping very nicely for herself and hers."

"You say you don't read many romance writers, other than your own," I said, rather disappointed with what I'd got from him so far. "Do you read Lorelei le Neve?"

He perked up immediately.

"Oh my, yes. Of course, everybody reads Lorelei. You've got to read her, analyse her appeal, if you're going to give any advice worth having to the aspirant writer. She just covers the spectrum—has an unerring instinct for the market, for people's weak spots, you might say. Added to which, we'd all like to be grooming a successor for Lorelei. Rumour has it about the publishing houses that she's a doomed woman."

"You don't actually know her?"

"Not personally."

"So you can't say anything about her as a human being?"

"You're using the phrase in its loosest sense, I hope. Well, no, though publishers do sometimes get together and gossip, you know. One hears things. And funnily enough, a sort of connection of mine did know her—or had dealings with her —long ago, before the war."

"A connection?"

"Actually a relative of my wife's."

"You have a wife?"

"Somewhere. This relative was manager of a factory that started up in Virginia, just before the war. It was government-aided, and the idea was that it could switch to war-production if necessary, which is what happened. Lorelei was personnel director. She was still quite young, but there can't be any mistake: that name is quite unique. It was at the end of the Depression, there were people who had been out of work the whole decade. Lorelei was responsible for hiring and firing. This uncle of my wife's said it was obscene, the joy she took in choosing who she hired and whom she fired. He said he'd never known anyone do it with such relish."

"No," I said. "I don't think there's been a mistake. That degree of relish for power is rare. Does he know anything about her subsequent career?"

"Not much. When war did come, she was a bit of an embarrassment: daughter of a fairly recent German immigrant family. As war production started up full employment returned, and the job lost its appeal. She was a trained singer, and she got herself hired by an opera company, for the chorus. This was Chicago, so far as I remember. She was a disruptive influence, always muscling in on any small parts going, and after a year or two she got the boot. At the end of the war she joined up. She hadn't been allowed to while hostilities lasted, but after '45 they found plenty of uses for German speakers. My impression is that she was in the armed services for quite a while."

"Anything more?"

"Not from him. As I say, one hears things in publishing circles . . . Apparently there was an English husband—one she chewed the bones of slowly, and then spat out. It was a process of slow breaking—I forgot whether he ended up as a suicide or a mental patient, or just flew the nest. As with Maryloo Parker, it was during the marriage that she started writing romances, I don't know whether it added savour to the breaking process, or perhaps it was part of it. Quite soon she began to earn well from it, moved back to New York, and since then it's been onwards and upwards."

"Nothing much to report about those years?"

"Some horrendous stories about how she treats fans. Not to mention how she treats editors. Of course, some of the fans ask for it, and not every editor is worth weeping for. On the business side at her publishers they're terrified of her, of course, and she makes the most ferocious bargains, or pushes her agent into making them. He's her puppet, and nothing but a dogsbody."

"I suppose her publishers are terrified of losing her?"

"Right. However much they squeak, eventually they cave in to the agent's demands. Actually she's had several agents, and split from them with acrimonious publicity. It's one hell of a life for whichever unlucky person it is at the moment."

"Know anything about this girl Felicity Maxwell?"

Marriott Dulac shrugged.

"Just a companion, I think. Wrote a couple of romances that were just about competent. Seems to be less bullied than you might expect, but from all accounts Lorelei is near death, so she may fear being left on her own. Though as far as the dying is concerned, it wouldn't surprise me if *that* was merely put around—by her, to get people pleasantly anticipating it, so she could get a bitter laugh out of disappointing them."

"It's an idea," I said. Seeing he had run down, I stood up, and he followed suit. "Well, it's been most interesting. All that about Lorelei conforms pleasantly to type. I think I'd be upset if I learned that she contributed to Spastics, or Dumb Animals, or even Cancer Research."

We went towards the foyer, through a maze of low, dimly-lighted, brown-carpeted corridors. Dulac seemed to be relapsing into his habitual obsession.

"Now what do I do? Follow up the chick I got half way with? Or try for something better? There's plenty here I could well think of going for a second round with. I suppose your Mary Sweeny wouldn't be around, would she?"

I was so surprised, because I had categorized the sort of women he was likely to go with, and certainly wouldn't have put Mary Sweeny in any of the categories, that I was for a moment speechless, and by the time I had thought of a question he was starting up the stairs with a wave of the hand. And I was prevented from going after him by a voice at my left hand, saying:

"Mr. Trethowan? Do you think we could talk?"

14

Best Friends

I turned. The speaker was a youngish woman, slim but wiry, almost without make-up, her hair clean but tangled. She had clearly been crying, but some time ago, and her expression suggested that she was now determined to face up to things bravely. Surely this must have been the female presence that I had been conscious of when I had been at the Scandilux Hotel earlier? But who was she? Her clothes told me nothing: they were about as nondescript and lacking in chic as it was possible to be—slacks, top, cardigan, shoes, all in a merely haphazard job-lot of colours: fawns, greys and muddy greens. But that, of course, marked her off from a great number of the delegates at the conference . . . Wait . . . Surely I *had* seen her before . . . And then there was that slight twang to the voice that even the few words she had spoken had revealed . . . Got it!

"Of course," I said. "You're the Australian publisher."

She gave me a lop-sided smile, that in other circumstances might have made her nondescript face almost pretty.

"That's a somewhat grand way of putting it. It was Amanda's way of putting it. Actually I'm on the staff of the Australian end of the Tamworth publishing group. I have general charge of the romance section. If anything, I'm Amanda's Australian editor, though of course I don't have to do much beyond suggesting words or phrases that have another meaning to an Australian reader, or situations or descriptions that an Australian reader might find offensive. There are more of those than you might think."

"I'm sure there are. Right. Well, it looks as if the sun is shining outside. Shall we go for a walk along the docks?"

The sun was indeed still shining, spreading liquid gold way out to sea. At the end of the promontory, the boat for England was in again, and we headed in its direction, threading our way past little boats and big, over ropes and round casks of fish, smelling the smells of a busy port.

"Right," I said. "I gather you know me, but as far as I'm concerned we need to be properly acquainted. You know—name, age, place of birth, all that kind of thing."

The formality seemed to perk her up.

"Name: Robyn Harben. Age: twenty-four years. Place of birth: Busselton in Western Australia. Occupation: tyro publisher. As you might have guessed, my job sounds more important than it actually is. I'm still very much learning the trade. Not that there *is* much of a publishing trade in Australia—though there's more than there was twenty years ago."

"You plan to branch out into British publishing?"

"I *did*. I hoped so—at least for a time. I wanted to get the experience of a really big operation, just for a while. Now, I don't know . . ."

"You've been wanting to talk to me all day, haven't you?"

"Yes."

"Because I'm investigating the death of Amanda?"

"Yes. And especially since I heard that the Norwegian police had been going round the various conference delegates, talking to everyone whose name was Robert."

Ah! I thought. Of course, I should have twigged it half a minute earlier. "Because you in fact are Robbie," I said.

"Yes," she said sadly. "I'm Robbie."

I wanted to let her have a minute or two's silence, so I turned away from the docks and we crossed the road towards the Rosenkrantz Tower and Håkonshallen, guarding the peninsula and dominating it. When we were safely within this mediaeval enclave, I said:

"Perhaps you'd better tell me how you got to know Amanda."

"Of course," she said, in her low voice as we strolled along through the tourists. "It's easily told. Though by the way, I always called her Maureen, or Mo. There weren't many people

who did that. They all knew, and yet she was
Amanda to everyone. She'd been swamped by
that silly role. And of course often she had to
play it while I was around. But when we were
alone . . ."

She was nearly weeping again, and we walked
on in silence, through the tower, and out on to
the little patches of lawn around the hall.

"You asked me something?" she said, putting
her hand to her forehead.

"How you got to know Amanda."

"Yes, sorry. She came to Australia on a publicity tour. Naturally. The romance-reading audience is about the most conservative in Australia.
They still prefer romances with a British background. They're the sort of reader who still re-
fers to Britain as 'Home.' Amanda is fantastically
popular there. She did signing sessions all the
way round from Western Australia to Queens-
land. In fact, she even had a signing stopover in
Darwin on the way home, though she wrote to
me later that it was like being beyond the
world's end. Western Australia's my home, and I
was with her from the beginning, up until
Townsville."

We sat down on the grass, and I let her think
and tell me about it in her own way. There was
something lost and childish about her, in spite of
the fact that she had chosen a lifestyle very different from that of most women, and one Aus-
tralians in particular were unlikely to look on
kindly or generously.

"I was very sceptical about her at first, naturally," she began. "I say naturally because of

course she was performing all the time, playing that silly role. The Australian side of the business was not—emphatically *not*—in on the secret. But one evening, over dinner in a dreadful hotel in Albany, she told me. Something . . . I don't know . . . clicked between us, and she told me. And from then on she could be herself with me, when we were together and out of the public eye. This made a bond between us . . ."

"What was the difference between 'Amanda' and 'Maureen'?" I asked.

"Chalk and cheese! I'm sure that was deliberate, so that when she was Amanda she was always consciously playing, and wouldn't slip back into herself. That was the big danger. Even so, I've noticed at this conference that sometimes she said things that were just too sharp and intelligent for that Amanda persona."

"I noticed that too."

"That may be because I've been there: even though we knew each other so well, she did often still feel the need to impress on me that she did have a brain, whatever appearances might suggest to the contrary. Or it might have been that the impersonation was wearing very thin. Amanda was fun to do at first—she often told me that she really enjoyed it, got a kick out of the silliness, and being *convincingly* silly— but you can see that it must have been tedious and demeaning after a time."

"You haven't told me what 'Maureen' was like."

"Oh—Mo was warm, witty, intelligent, and very interested in other people. That's why she

could conduct such a good battle with that
Sørby woman—she got her summed up very
quickly, and she could attack her on her weakest
points: her egotism, her delusions and generalizations about women. Mo would have made a
good politician, and I mean that as a compli-
ment. No, Mo was a marvellous person, and one
hardly anyone knew about."

"Except her . . . friends," I hinted.

"Yes."

"How did that come about?"

"Inevitably, I suppose you could say. You
know how it is in Australia—oh, perhaps you
don't. Well, if you're any kind of celebrity, every
town you go to you have to give interviews: the
local radio and television stations, the press, everything. And if you don't, the media are into
you with sabres flashing, and that really is a
charge of the heavy brigade. Then it's on to the
next town, and the same round, the same questions, and so on. Amanda was a great catch and a
good interviewee, but naturally she got exhausted. I changed the plan so that I drove her
everywhere—from radio station to TV station
and back to the hotel for the newspaper journal-
ists and the woman from *Woman's Weekly*. That
meant that at least we were alone in the car, and
for that time we could be ourselves. Soon, if we
were in a decent hotel, we started eating in our
bedrooms, so as to be alone. What followed just
. . . came naturally from that."

"Amanda was already a lesbian?"

Robbie Harben opened her eyes wide.

"But of course. This was only two or three

years ago. She had had hetero affairs too, but predominantly she was a lesbian. There had been no one big affair, but she had a circle in Britain—just a few younger women, with whom she could be natural. Of course, they all knew about her double life—or else some just knew her as Maureen, and knew nothing of Amanda, though that was rare, since she was quite often on television."

"So what happened when the publicity tour ended?"

"We said goodbye. That was always the arrangement."

"And since?"

"I had three weeks in Britain last year. We went touring in Wales and Ireland. It was heaven. We were not 'in love,' you know; just deeply fond of each other. And we were going to have some days together after the conference ended."

"I know. And you had managed . . . time together since this conference began?"

My hesitation gave her the clue to what I was talking about, and after a moment she nodded.

"I was out once to the guest-house. Heavenly place. I went out the second evening, and Amanda met the bus. But mostly we were saving that for when we went up into the mountains after all this junketing is finished."

"If you went out to the guest-house, she may have talked to you about the other delegates staying there."

"She did talk about them. I don't remember whether it was then or some other time."

"She didn't feel that any of them had a grudge against her—she wasn't *afraid*?"

"Good heavens, no. Anyway, Mo was never afraid. And there was no reason why she should be—at least, none that she was aware of, otherwise she would have told me."

"What and who did she tell you about, then?"

"That she was playing this tremendous game with Lorelei le Neve. This mock rivalry. She was enjoying that: it appealed to the actress in her. Losing gave her an even better part than winning. She said that Lorelei has a power obsession, and that if Lorelei won the game she could watch the obsession swelling her up, like a frog. She said Arthur Biggs had the same sort of obsession."

"Did she, though?"

"Only secretly: she said he liked covert, underground power, whereas Lorelei would flaunt hers. He liked knowing things, and using them. Apparently he'd done something of that sort with the Amanda Fairchild impersonation."

"He had—that's right."

"She said that was the only way he knew of conducting relationships . . . What else? She said there was a nice little woman called Mary Sweeny who had written Amanda Fairchild books."

"What?"

"Books or book, I forget which. Early ones, anyway. She had two tremendously professional ladies who do all of them now, and she'd met both of them."

"She didn't say any more about Mary Sweeny?"

"No—just that." She sat there twisting her handkerchief for a minute or two, and looking up at me, and then she added: "Another thing that Amanda said—forgive me—was that you had a dim little sister here, but that you were more sharp, and she kept giving herself away in front of you."

"Chrissy's not as dim as she seems," I protested loyally. Then honesty compelled me to ruin the gesture by adding: "Though nearly. Anything else?"

"No . . . No, I don't think so . . ." She brushed a hand over her eyes, and together we got up and wandered out through the Rosenkrantz Tower (surely Shakespeare's Rosencrantz could never have managed to build a tower?), and out into the sun-littered streets along Bryggen. "But you will remember, won't you," Robyn said, "that she wasn't stupid, and she wasn't pretentious or bitchy?"

"I never thought she was stupid," I said. "Or anyway, not after the first evening. She always puzzled me."

"She wasn't perfect. But she was clever, and funny, and very, very sharp."

"She wasn't sharp enough not to make that assignation," I said. "Do you know anything about that?"

"No. Had she made it when she was with me on the bus, in the afternoon?"

"I don't know. Probably the *note* came later: there was a very brief one, naming a time. But this almost certainly must have been a follow-up to something that had been suggested, or tentatively arranged earlier. I thought she might have mentioned something about it to you."

"No . . . And yet, if it had been talked of, I think she would have told me. We talked about everything, you know, while we were together."

We were back at the Scandilux, and we stood for a moment outside the main entrance.

"That's all," I said. "If there's anything else I think of, I'll give you a ring."

"Will you solve it?" she asked.

"Yes, I'll solve it. Whether I'll solve it in such a way that a case can be brought, I'm less sure. The more time passes, the less easy that becomes. You go in, and get something out of the rest of the conference. You'll have other friends."

"But I'll never have another—Amanda," she said, and dipped into the dark of the foyer.

The view over the water towards the main part of Bergen, with the little church with the onion dome in the middle of the land mass, was so entrancing that I stood there in the late sun, drinking it in, revelling in the dappled lemon light on the water. As I stood there, breathing in the fresh, hard Norwegian air, I saw coming along the quay from the market Auberon Lawrence, in his element—with a romantic novelist on each arm. He was chortling and shrilling and patting their hands, and they were twittering and making up to him as only authors can make up to their publishers. It seemed a shame to break things up, but when they crossed the road I put myself in front of him and he drew in his breath and regarded me blankly, as if I were some sort of apparition from the future—a child crowned, or an armed head.

"Could I have a word?" I said.

"Oh dear—if you must. Wait for me, dear ladies!" he exhorted them, as they went through the swing doors into the darkness of the foyer. I had always wanted to meet someone who said "dear lady," and now I had I could forget it. He was really very cross with me. "Is it important? Those are two of my sweetest writers!"

"Not very important, but I wanted to verify something. Did you know that Amanda Fairchild was a lesbian?"

He shrugged.

"Yes."

"Why didn't you tell me?"

"Oh dear, why should I? I hate labels. He's black, he's white, she's straight, she's bent. We're all blackish and whitish, straightish and bentish. People can't be card-indexed."

"Point taken," I said. "But you did know that, from time to time, she engaged in lesbian activities?"

"Yes. But she did it very discreetly, so we didn't think it any affair of ours. It didn't affect the impersonation."

"Did she have one main friend?"

"Oh no, I don't think so. Just a lot of quiet friendships that she kept up with over a long period. At least, that was the pattern until this Australian girl came along. That seemed to be more serious. She actually begged for a job for her with our Australian branch, and of course she's here now."

"I see . . . I think I see . . . How in the straightish/bentish scale would you categorize Amanda?"

"Dear boy, how would I *know*? We didn't bump into each other socially." He cast longing glances into the murk of the foyer. "Oh well, if you want a guess—I'd say seventy-five bent to twenty-five straight."

"I see," I said. That was about all I did see. I didn't see why Robyn Harben had lied about her job. I didn't see why Amanda had confided in her about the impersonation, I didn't see what Robyn had been meaning to say with her last words before she vanished into the hotel. But about Amanda's lesbian nature, at least, she seemed to be telling the truth.

15
The Wilder Shores

When I got back to Kvalevåg it was past dinner-time. It was also, according to Stein and Svein, time to question the Finn. I did wonder if they were right. It must have been about three when he was locked in his new bedroom. It was now only half past eight. The Finn had been drinking solidly since he had arrived at Kvalevåg. Indeed, he gave every sign of having been drinking solidly for weeks, months, years before that—vodka-sodden aeons in the invigorating chill of the passing Finnish seasons. What chance had five or six hours against such a long, pickled adulthood?

At first when we opened the door it seemed as though I was right. Svein went in first, with Stein behind him, and both found themselves the objects of a howling, incoherent attack—the gaunt, enraged Finn throwing himself upon them, clutching at the scruff of Svein's neck and throwing ill-directed but vicious punches in Stein's direction. Svein's experience with

Bergen's drunks proved equal to the occasion: within ten seconds he had him helpless against the wall, and more than a little tearful. Then Stein came up as close as he cared to get, promised him that if he would bath or shower, put on clean clothes, then come and be interviewed—after that he could go back to his old room. A tiny sparkle came to Martti's bloodshot eyes: he nodded, wiped his eyes, and was led off to the bathroom by the stalwart sergeant who had guarded his room before. Soon we heard the sound of much water being run for a bath.

Coming into the room, I could smell why they had insisted on that: the room reeked of stale alcohol and sweat. We opened the windows and let in the glorious Norwegian evening air. We talked about the Finn a bit, and I tried to articulate something that had been at the back of my mind.

"Remember," I said, with that touch of didacticism that is one of my besetting sins, "that he did take those trips to the lavatory, and probably no one would have noticed if he was a fair bit longer than most people usually are when they go to the loo. They would assume subconsciously that he was taking a long time getting there, or getting back, or maybe that he was throwing up. Remember Wes and Felicity and la Zuckerman had all been drinking themselves, so they're far from perfect witnesses."

"But the fact that he was drunk *would* mean that he would take twice as long as anyone else to get around," objected Svein. "Quite apart from the question whether he could have drowned Amanda at all in that condition."

"*If* he was drunk," I amended. "You can smell like a brewery and still be perfectly sober. You can soak your clothes in it. It's as easy to act a stage drunk as it is to act a stage Irishman. In fact, looking at some of your Bergen drunks, they remind me of nothing so much as silent film drunks. Imitating one of them would be a piece of cake. All I'm saying is that we should take nothing for granted."

While I had been talking, something had clicked in my mind—some connection, some neglected fact. When I had finished talking, it had gone, gone beyond recall. Yet . . . there it niggled, still at the back there. Surely it would come back, eventually . . . Meanwhile there was a click of a door from the bathroom along the corridor, and a few seconds later Martti Leino walked in.

It was for the first time possible to consider him as a man. A drunk is just a drunk, he neither rises nor falls to being a person, but a person was what stood before us. Stein and Svein had been quite right about how long it would take him to sober up, but then, they were the ones with the experience of Scandinavian drunks. Martti Leino was rather above average height, cadaverous of face and body, white of skin and with oddly colourless hair that would have been classified as blond, yet was not. His features must once have been strong, even impressive, but self-indulgence had covered them with blotchy, unhealthy skin, and the eyes were cloudy and largely unfocused. But there was no doubt that he was all there, was following things, and had become a real man. Though a decidedly unhappy one.

"Christ," he said blackly. "Do you have the right to do that?"

He sat down, put his head in his hands, then peeked out and looked around as if he expected us to have brought in a bar.

"We do," said Stein equably. "Do you imagine that you have some sort of constitutional or God-given right to be drunk twenty-four hours a day?"

"Yes," said Martti simply. "If I can afford it."

"Are you always as drunk as this?"

"If I have the money. When I haven't, I sober up and write a few books. Then I get drunk again."

"Why?" I asked. He obviously thought it a silly question.

"Why not? It's a way of life. Other people kill themselves with cigarettes, or jogging. Me—I drink."

"Did you start drinking because your wife left you?" asked Stein, in tones of sympathy.

"Something like that. Or maybe the other way round. No Finn knows when or why he started drinking. What are you so interested in that for?"

We all sighed, and Stein took off on another tack.

"How drunk were you on the night of the murder?"

Martti shrugged.

"Pretty much as usual."

"Do you remember what you talked about in Mrs. Zuckerman's room?"

He screwed up his face and shook his head.

"Nothing?"

"Nothing."

"Do you remember who was there?"

"That fat old cow in purple, whatever name that was you just said. Her little nurse . . . someone else . . . Oh, that guy from India or somewhere like that."

"Kenya."

"That's it. That isn't India?"

"No."

"I must try and remember that."

"While you were drinking with that lot, you went out to the lavatory."

"I imagine so."

"You don't remember?"

"For Chrissake, don't you realize how often I go to the lavatory in the course of the day? Of course I don't remember."

"Nor how often you went, how long it took?"

"No. Full stop. NO."

It really was very difficult to know what to ask him.

"The others went out from time to time," Stein pressed on.

"I think so. Not the big purple cow, though. She sat there in her . . . barn."

"You're sure of that? You noticed the whole time?"

"Oh no. I went to sleep now and then. But she's crippled, and she couldn't get around."

It was enough to make you weep. Stein merely sighed, a quiet, delicate, Norwegian little sigh.

"And the others?"

"The Indian went out. I know that."

"Kenyan. Yes, we know. Do you remember anything about his going out? How long he was away, for instance?"

Martti shook his head.

"When am I getting this drink?"

"In a minute," Stein said. He signalled surreptitiously to the stalwart sergeant to go and fetch a bottle from Leino's stock, the collection of twelve half-bottles found under the floorboards in his old bedroom.

"And Miss Maxwell?"

"She fetched the drinks."

"Did she take especially long over it?"

"Yes."

"Which time?"

"Every time. I was waiting."

This time we all three sighed, very audibly.

"Well, I'm not used to waiting between drinks," Martti protested. "It makes me nervous. I like the new one on the table as soon as I've finished the old one." His eyes lit up as the sergeant came in with a half-bottle of Smirnoff. "*And* once the bitch brought me the wrong brand. It's *only* Smirnoff for me. Can I have one? Can I have a little drink?"

"Well," said Stein reluctantly, "we can't get less out of you than we've got so far."

Martti Leino grabbed at the bottle, wrenched at the screw top, and then threw back his head and the bottle at the same time and consumed, neat, a good third of the contents. As he came to, shaking his head at the impact, Stein took the bottle from his unwary hand, and managed to avoid Martti's feet as he kicked out.

"For when we've finished," Stein said.

"Oh, come on, come on," said Martti urgently. "There's nothing more to tell. I've told you everything."

"How were you sitting in Mrs. Zuckerman's room?"

"*Christ!* . . . she was in front, facing us, like she was some sort of teacher . . . Then we were around her—me in the armchair closest to the window, then the Indian in the other armchair, then the little nurse over on the desk chair."

"Could you see all the other three?"

"Of course I could—when I was awake."

"What did you talk about?"

"Markets. I wasn't interested in that. No one's going to translate Finnish romances for the American market. Then trends. That was a bit more interesting. You can get ideas . . . Not that the Finnish market is the same as the international." He made a little circle with his thumb and third finger, to indicate Finland's uniqueness. "Finland is absolutely on its own!"

He made a lunge in the direction of the bottle, but Stein passed it deftly from one hand to the other behind his chair, and put up his knee in Martti's path. He retired badly winded, and in a very black mood. Stein and Svein really seemed to have valuable expertise in dealing with people like Martti.

"Don't try that again," Stein said. "I'm the one who decides when you have your next drink. So did this talk of markets and trends go on all evening?"

"Pretty much so, as far as I remember . . . Then later on, there was noise outside . . . screaming."

"So what did you do?"

"Took no notice at first. Went on talking. Then we heard a lot of voices from the lawn. The girl goes to the window. 'I think something's happened,' she says, and she goes out on to the balcony. The window is really a little door, and their sitting-room has the small round balcony in the centre of the house. She calls down to someone in the grounds, and then shouts in to us: 'I think somebody's dead.' It's only a little tiny balcony, so I leave the room, because my drink was dry and there was no sign of getting another. I collect a half-bottle from my room, and I go downstairs and out to the porch and watch from there."

"That's right," I said. "I saw him."

"Now," said Stein, speeding up his questionnaire, apparently knowing that this was a crucial time in the Finn's progression from sobriety to haziness, "you went out of the room to go to the lavatory. When? What time?"

"Don't know," said Martti, faltering. "DON'T KNOW."

"What about the others? Miss Maxwell, for example."

"She went to fetch drinks. When my glass was empty I started jiggling it—to remind her, subtly. Three times she did that—once for me alone, otherwise for her and the Indian as well."

"Did she take a long time?"

"Too bloody long. But that's that woman behind the bar. She doesn't approve of people drinking, even though she makes enough money out of it, and she goes slow when she's getting the drinks, so you can sober up between. It's a bloody scandal."

Now I came to think about it, I realized that Martti was right. He had a drinker's perspicacity in matters affecting his drinking. Stein said: "What about the Kenyan?"

"Wes, his name is," said Martti, the first time he had used it. "Bloody silly name. What's it short for? Westminster? He went out . . . yes, he went out."

"He went out to the lavatory," said Stein, gently prodding.

"Yes, he did. . . . But he went out for something else too . . . What was it? . . . He came back with something too . . . Books, that's what it was . . ."

"We know that."

"His own books, because he started showing them round . . . Wouldn't be much good me showing *my* books around, would it? . . . But there was something funny . . . something funny . . ."

We kept very quiet, as Martti's brain struggled.

"Where did he get the books from? Eh? Where did he get them from?"

"From his room, I suppose," said Stein quietly.

"But he didn't! Because when you go out of Lorelei's sitting-room, his room is five doors down to the right. And he didn't go off to the right. He went to the left, and came back from the left. Where did he get them from, then?"

Stein handed him his half-bottle of Smirnoff.

16

Ganging Up

We finished with Martti and left him with his bottle. Stein expressed some satisfaction: "It often happens like that," he said, with the wisdom born of experience. I left them to various routine jobs that for once I felt I could keep away from, and I took myself off downstairs in search of food. Unfortunately I got no farther than the lounge, where I found the suspects— even unto Cristobel and Bernard—assembled and deep in *sotto voce* talk. Some held drinks and some held pens and paper, and it was obvious that they had been collectively doing something or other which they conceived as of great importance. It was Cristobel who spoke, and I suspected that she had been deputed to do so.

"Perry," she said, "do you think we could all have a talk with you?"

"All of you? At once?"

"Well, yes, actually," said Bernard.

"Ah—well, I have to scavenge in search of

food. I haven't had anything to eat since breakfast."

"Dinner is over," said Cristobel, with that
ruthlessness which is one of her fortes, and one
of her inheritances from our loathsome family.
"You won't be able to get anything now."

"Fru Tønnesen is as anxious as any of you to
get this business sorted out," I said. "I'm sure she
won't want the inner man of one of the investi-
gators to be crying out in hunger all night."

"Well, you can bring your meal *up here*," said
Cristobel, in that voice which, if I had been Bernard, would have held ominous warnings for
me.

"I will come up after I have eaten," I said
firmly. Food and the exercise of the razor-sharp
intellect do not go together.

Fru Tønnesen was behind the bar, but she
closed it down with the greatest of readiness—
confirming Martti's dire suspicions—in order to
put together something for me. We went into
the kitchen, and she carved great slices of beef,
ham and chicken, and served it with potato
salad, tomatoes, cucumber and bread and but-
ter. In my famished state it seemed like a feast,
and I ate it in the deserted dining-room—a more
comfortable meal than I had ever had there
hitherto, what with the looming presence of
Lorelei and all the other embarrassments. As I
ate I was turning over in my mind all the little
hints and indications which I had been storing
up in all the interviews I had had since Amanda
died. I even made, for my own satisfaction, a list
of possible suspects: I included all the other

guests at the *Kvalevåg Gjestgiveri*, including the Bavarians and the American family; of the hotel staff I included Fru Tønnesen and her nephew Gorm, since I knew the rest had gone home before the crucial time; there were Everard Manning and Bernard Palterton, who were there as guests; and at the end I added Robyn Harben and Ragnhild Sørby. By these last two names I wrote: "Could they?" then, after thought, I added: "Yes."

I was not particularly anxious, you notice, to go upstairs. I suspected they had been cooking something up—indeed the smell of cooking penetrated even down here to the dining-room.

"Perry, we've been thinking," said my sister, when at last, with evident reluctance, I went up again to the lounge. Typically, she said it at the moment I set toe within the lounge area. Beating about the bush is frowned upon in the Girl Guides.

All the possible replies to her attack seemed to smack of the obvious, so I merely raised my eyebrows.

"In fact, we've been making out a time chart," said Arthur Biggs, who was sitting with wife and friend in the familiar triangle, but who this time was clearly also part of the bunch. "A time chart of our movements on the evening of the murder."

That seemed not altogether a bad idea, but I was loath to express appreciation of anything Biggs had a hand in.

"Are your memories precise enough to make

that worth while?" I asked, with an appearance of scepticism.

"We think so," said Biggs, "though obviously you have to allow for a few minutes either way much of the time."

"And we remember rather less than the rest," said Bernard, with what I took to be scrupulous honesty, his arm around Cristobel to show he meant him and her.

"I've got the table here, if you'd like to take a look at it," said Patti Drewe. "It covers the period from the time Amanda came down to the bar, to the time we heard your sister—"

"Doing her nut," said Bernard, looking at her affectionately.

"Fair enough," I said, taking it. There were in fact two sheets, one of which dealt with the crucial time chronologically, the other of which noted the movements of most of the hotel's guests who were part of the Romantic Novelists' Conference. I had to admit it seemed a sensible and methodical way of proceeding. And when I studied the first page, I had to admit that on the surface they seemed to have done a good and convincing job.

TIMETABLE

7:20: Dinner finishes.

7:45: Peregrine Trethowan and Amanda Fairchild to bar. A.F. returns to her room (unvouched for until 9:10). P.T. joins tables in bar with Wes Mackay, Martti Leino, Patti Drewe, Mary Sweeny and Maryloo Parker. At other tables: Arthur and Selina Biggs, Everard Manning; party of Germans, party of Americans.

7:55:   Wes Mackay and Martti Leino to Lorelei Zuckerman's room.

8:45:   Cristobel Trethowan and Bernard Palterton proceed from grounds to road.

9:05:   Peregrine Trethowan from bar to telephone in lounge.

9:10:   Amanda Fairchild down stairs and out into grounds. Bernard Palterton and Cristobel Trethowan on seat at far side of lawn, looking towards road.

9:20:   Peregrine Trethowan finishes phone call. Talks to Cristobel Trethowan and Bernard Palterton.

9:25:   Maryloo Parker to ladies' room. Back in bar by 9:30.

9:30:   Everard Manning to gents' room. Passes Maryloo Parker returning.

9:35:   A. Biggs to gents' room. Manning and he back by 9:37.

9:40:   Peregrine Trethowan to bar again. Various parties begin to mingle together.

9:45:   Mary Sweeny to ladies' room. Back by 9:50.

10:00:   All in Romantic party upstairs to lounge. Cristobel Trethowan and Bernard Palterton down to boathouse.

10:05:   Body found.

They all looked at me expectantly.

"Excellent," I said heartily. "Couldn't have been better done. How reliable is it?"

They all started talking at once. It was absolutely reliable, they'd worked at it, and checked and counter-checked, and I could be sure it was completely spot-on.

"Ah," I said. "So when I read here that Maryloo Parker went to the ladies' room at 9:25 and was back by 9:30, I can be quite sure that that is what happened?"

"Yes, truly!" said Patti Drewe. "Mary and I both remember that she wasn't gone more than five minutes *at most*, and Everard Manning passed her as she was on her way back."

"And when Mary Sweeny went to the ladies' later on, I can be quite sure she was only there for five minutes?"

"Oh, absolutely," said Maryloo Parker. "Patti and I are quite certain. Five minutes at the outside."

"Funny. I was down in the bar then, but I can neither remember her leaving the room, nor how long she was away. You must all have remarkably good memories."

"Some people *do* have better memories than others," Mary Sweeny protested.

"Yes. Policemen, to name but one group. Good to know that romantic writers train themselves to an even greater accuracy. But now Mr. Manning, I see, was away for all of *seven* minutes."

"But certainly not longer, Superintendent," said Arthur Biggs, in his university-lecturer voice. "That I can vouch for, and so can my wife—"

"Oh yes, absolutely," fluted Mrs. Biggs in concert.

"—and anyway seven minutes is not long enough to . . . to do what was done, is it?"

"It might not be," I admitted. "On the other hand, it is quite a long time for a man to spend in the lavatory."

"I have an upset stomach," said Everard Manning, trying to maintain his minor-but-mildly-distinguished-author look, though in fact it was much more an upset-tummy look, when I came to think about it. "I've had it since I got here. I don't think the food agrees with me. Or maybe it's the water."

"The water is about as pure as you're likely to find anywhere in the world," I pointed out. "Is it the lack of chlorine that affects you so badly? And I really can't imagine pork chops or boiled fish playing havoc with anybody's tummy." I added, rather sharply: "Come off it. You're not in bloody Marrakesh . . . Actually, that sequence of visits to the loo strikes me as a little odd. *While* Mr. Manning is still away, Mr. Biggs also goes, leaving his wife alone at the table."

Arthur Biggs looked at me mystified.

"Wouldn't one usually wait till the other person at the table returned?" I suggested. "So that your wife had someone to talk to?"

"But I wanted to go," said Arthur Biggs, uncomprehending.

"I didn't mind at all, really," twittered Mrs. Biggs.

"Oh well, let it go," I said. It was too late in the day to try and teach Arthur Biggs drinkers' manners. "And who is it who remembers that Mr. Biggs was only away two minutes?"

"Well, actually me," said Selina Biggs, a little confused. "Because I do remember I was alone only for a *terribly* short time."

"Hmmm," I said. "One thing does strike me about this beautiful catalogue of events. That is that all those of you who were down there in the bar do put each other beautifully in the clear. It's quite touching how much notice you all took of each other. Whereas none of you seems to have noticed Felicity Maxwell's visits to the bar or how long they were. And out in the garden Cristobel and Bernard—"

"You mustn't blame them for that," Cristobel protested. "It's our fault. We were just . . . wandering around."

A sort of galumphing coyness came over Cristobel at this point, and I almost felt she exaggerated her ignorance of where they were at any point in the evening to underline the romantic nature of their long interview.

"She's right," said Bernard, just as bad. "We were going from place to place. And apart from going to talk to the boy who was standing waiting at the road, and then later telling you about the accident, we don't actually remember where we were at any one time."

"The trouble with fall guys," I said, "is that they are usually all too pathetically ready to fall."

"That's absolutely uncalled for," said Arthur

Biggs hotly—or at any rate vaguely pepperishly. "In fact, you'll find that the other sheet sets it all out perfectly fairly."

"Ah—no doubt," I said. And there, indeed, it all was.

MOVEMENTS

ARTHUR BIGGS:	in bar, except for very short visit to gents' room, 9:35.
EVERARD MANNING:	in bar except for short visit to ditto, 9:30.
SELINA BIGGS:	in bar whole time.
MARY SWEENY:	in bar except for short visit to ladies' room, 9:45.
MARYLOO PARKER:	in bar except for short visit to ditto, 9:25.
PATTI DREWE:	in bar whole time.
WES MACKAY:	in bar until 7:55. Then Lorelei Zuckerman's room. One visit to second-floor lavatory, one visit to own room for books.
MARTTI LEINO:	in bar until 7:55. Then Lorelei Zuckerman's room except for two visits to sec-

	ond-floor lava-tory.
CRISTOBEL TRETHOWAN:	together in
BERNARD PALTERTON:	grounds whole time. Talked to boy from the guest-house *ca* 8:45–9:05. Talked to Peregrine Trethowan *ca* 9:20.

"Very clearly set out," I said. "You have missed out the Zuckerman ménage, I see."

"They have not been much in communication with us," said Mary Sweeny, "not since the murder. So we felt we couldn't do it reliably."

"I see. I do sense a slight slant against the Zuckerman room on the night in question, even without an account of the ladies' movements. While the visits to the loo of those in the bar are always 'short,' when they are not 'very short,' those of Mr. Mackay and Mr. Leino are always of unspecified duration."

"That's because we couldn't get independent verification," drawled Maryloo Parker. "That's why we had to leave the activities of your sister and her . . . Mr. Palterton vague: they thought they might have been here or there, at this or that time, but apart from the talk with you, and the chat with the boy from here, there was no independent verification."

"No-o," I said. "Except that Bernard vouching for Cristobel and Cristobel vouching for Bernard seems to me quite as valuable as Mrs. Biggs vouching for Mr. Biggs."

There was a little squawk of protest, presumably from Mrs. Biggs, though possibly from Mr. Biggs. I heard Cristobel say, in her slow way: "I suppose that's true, isn't it?" I rolled the two sheets of paper into a tube, and tapped them in irritation on the back of a chair.

"You do realize, don't you, that these things that you've concocted are next to valueless?"

"They're not!" protested Maryloo. "They're very accurate, and properly witnessed."

"They establish one thing fairly conclusively: that you, Mrs. Biggs, and you, Mrs. Drewe, could not have done it, having been in the bar the whole time. I think, you know, that I could have established that quite easily by dint of a little questioning. Otherwise—you've just got together in cosy cahoots, and said 'yes' to whatever each other says about movements. A says, 'I went to the loo,' and B says, 'Oh yes, I remember,' and A says, 'I wasn't five minutes—probably less,' and B says, 'Oh no, I'm sure you weren't longer than five minutes.' That's how reliable it all is. Don't think you can pull the wool over my eyes. I've been in bars, I've been in loos. No one remembers how long people take. They *may* remember if they were away an especially long time—though even then their evidence won't be as reliable as a sober person's. But there's too much drinking, too much talking, too much going on generally, for anyone to be as definite as you've made them. I really don't believe in B looking at her watch just when A goes to the loo, and remembering afterwards that she did so, and what the watch said. And looking again when A comes back. Keep that sort of thing for the story books."

"I think you're being unduly cynical," said Mary Sweeny. "You're not making allowances for the fact that there are lots of different *sorts* of memory—and some kinds remember these insignificant details as well."

"*And* you're being ungrateful, to boot," said Maryloo.

"Ungrateful?" I said, mystified. "What have I got to be grateful for?"

"The fact that we missed out of our survey the most suspicious thing of all."

"What was that?"

"The fact that between 9:25 and 9:40 your own movements are entirely unaccounted for."

17

False Witnesses

I spent a troubled, restless night, and it wasn't
due to uneasiness over the snide suggestion of
Maryloo Parker. I knew I hadn't killed Amanda
Fairchild—was confident, even, that I had not
suddenly become a schizophrenic whose darker
half had nipped off down to the boathouse to
polish off Amanda between phoning Jan and returning to the bar. I was pretty confident, too,
that (whatever some of that lot down there
might think) no one in their senses would consider I had a motive for putting an end to la
Fairchild.

The trouble was, I couldn't see that any of the
others had much more of a motive than I had.

Other things were beginning to sort themselves out a little, to take on some sort of pattern.
But motive . . . The whole thing was beset by
too many false trails, too much lying, too much
concealing. These people pretended to be so
straightforward and open, yet even the fact of
Amanda's impersonation would not have come

out if I had not wiggled it out—and that was a fact known to at least two, and I would guess probably four, of the people on my suspect list. As to the other, lesser lies and concealments, they were legion. I arose with a black, misanthropic hatred of all these people. How right I had been in the first place, when Cristobel first broached the matter, not to want to come among them!

I went down late to breakfast. This time they couldn't avoid me even if they wanted to, for I fetched a vast plate of this and that, and sat down in the midst of them to eat it. To be fair, they showed no signs of shunning me. As they ate or sipped their coffee, they threw quick, birdlike glances in my direction, and then looked back at their plates.

This time it was Wes Mackay who led the attack.

"Are you any forrarder this morning?"

I shrugged.

"Forrarder by a night's thought."

"Is that night's thought going to get us out of this unofficial custody any the quicker?"

"I'm less worried about you getting out than about me getting out, but still—it might, it might."

"What's the substance of your thinking?"

"That an awful lot of you are barefaced liars."

There ought to have been a great outburst of protestations at this, but there was only a little apoplectic sound like a popping of a champagne cork from Arthur Biggs. Otherwise they did no more than suck in outraged breaths, or in some cases look down at the tablecloth. They knew my opinion of them already. And they knew they were liars before I told them.

"Since you've already acknowledged," said Patti Drewe, "that I couldn't have done it—"

"I've done no such thing. I've acknowledged that you were in the bar for what was apparently the crucial time."

"Well, that's enough for me. So I can ask: what lies have been told by us here?"

I could feel several people wanting to shush her, and holding back with difficulty.

"About you I have to admit I know nothing," I said, turning to Patti. "Some of the others, too, I have no black marks against: Mr. Leino, for example, in so far as he has told me anything, seems to have told the truth. Most of you, however, have certainly either concealed something, or lied about something."

I somewhat melodramatically jabbed my fork in the direction of Mary Sweeny, who neither jumped nor looked innocent, but continued looking at me in a stoic fashion that I thought did her credit.

"You for a start have lied about your knowledge of the Amanda Fairchild impersonation. You've known about it for years. You wrote one of the early books published under her name."

She nodded, still not obviously discomposed.

"Yes—that's true. It was published in 1967."

"So all you've said about Amanda and her books—we talked about them in the bus coming out here, I remember, and you waxed fairly eloquent—was lies."

"Obviously I'd prefer some other word. Such as playing along with the fiction. Doing that was part of the agreement I made with the Tamworth group, the publishers. And I always got a lot of quiet fun from my knowledge."

"You didn't also have a lot of quiet resentment towards the woman who had profited by your writing?"

"I did not. Why should I? Going by Amanda's nearness with money, I would guess that she didn't profit that much. If I were inclined to indulge in resentment—which I am not—it would be the publishers I would fix on, not Amanda. But in fact the publishers and I came to an agreement, it was for me a perfectly satisfactory agreement, and I stuck to it. I felt no resentment for her, and was never tempted for a moment to give her away."

"Not even to Marriott Dulac?" I said nastily.

"Marriott Dulac?" A slow, reminiscent smile spread over her face. "I really don't think so. We did have so much else of more interest to talk about and do. Marriott Dulac is rather a special sort of man."

"You can say that again," said Maryloo Parker, and she actually rubbed her hands. How shocked Ragnhild Sørby would have been!

"Yes," I said, "I rather suspect that your account to me when we first met of Marriott Dulac's relationship to romantic woman writers was slanted if not inaccurate. You rather played up the grab on his part, and played down the throwing themselves on their part."

"That sort of slanting has always been one of a woman's privileges," said Maryloo coyly.

"Quite. And however hard I strain I can't see that the matter of both of you sleeping with a publisher is of relevance—even conceivable relevance—to Amanda's death. Arthur Biggs's misrepresentations, on the other hand, seem rather closer to the centre of the matter."

"Misrepresentations?" Biggs said in an airy way, though snappiness seemed to underlie his tone. "I haven't misrepresented anything. You guessed from my book that the figure of Amanda was a fake and a fraud, and I confirmed the guess—in so far as I was able."

"But in fact you were able to a much greater extent than you admitted, weren't you? You knew the full extent of the publishers' little game, because in fact you have used your knowledge to blackmail yourself on to her publisher's list. That was the initial use you made of your knowledge. No doubt you used it subsequently to screw better terms out of them than your reputation as Lorinda Mason would warrant, to get more promotion and publicity than they'd otherwise be inclined to give you. You were more than cagey about that. You didn't even admit that you shared a publisher with Amanda."

Arthur Biggs shrugged.

"It didn't seem relevant. And I may say—" he swelled a little at this, with distinct resemblances to a sandy and insignificant bullfrog— "that my books are held in very much higher esteem than you seem to think."

"As witness the tribute to them in your *Happy Tears*, paid to you by your friend Mr. Manning. Well, I think I know how to estimate that at its true worth. And by the way, I don't believe for a moment that your wife and friend did not know the Amanda impersonation. Clearly you wouldn't tell many people, otherwise your hold over the publishers would be weakened; but those are two you would tell, presenting it as a matter of suspicion, not of certainty. You wouldn't be able to hide your cleverness in detection from them."

Everard Manning shook his handsome, greased head vigorously, but Mrs. Briggs looked down, embarrassed, at the tablecloth.

"There are other people who have lied, and quite unnecessarily," I went on. "One of them is Robyn Harben, Amanda's Australian editor." I pushed my plate aside, without much regret, for all it now contained was a piece of the blandest cheese I had ever tasted in my life. "But the liar that I would like to talk to now is you, Mr. Mackay."

He looked up jerkily, but it was clear that he had been steeling himself against this. I got up from the table, and gestured him out in advance. He went up the stairs to the lounge, his whole body expressing a disastrous draining away of confidence. When we got to the lounge he looked at me inquiringly, and I gestured up the stairs again. No cosy chats around the crocuses for us today. This was, after all, the biggest liar of the lot. We went upstairs without speaking, then along to my bedroom. I thought I'd get more out of him without the presence of Stein and Svein. I sat him in the armchair, squatted on the bed myself, and looked at him in what I hoped was an intimidating manner.

"Now we'll talk about all your lies," I said.

"Concealments," he conceded.

"Lies by implication. Let me make clear what I know. I know you and she have slept together since you arrived here. I know you went along to her room on the night of the murder. I know your acquaintanceship dates from way back—I would suspect from back in the 1960s—early on in them too. Am I right?"

"You're right. 1961," he admitted, with frank admiration on his face. "Though how the hell you can know that—"

"Just tell it to me straight from the beginning. Then I might be able to tell you things that even you don't know."

"Well, we met when she was on a British Council drama tour, playing Lady Macduff and Celia in *As You Like It*."

"That's what I guessed."

"But how *did* you guess? Did she leave anything about me behind in her papers?"

"No. There was someone else here—it's a hell of a coincidence—someone else who saw her on that tour."

"Maybe it's not so much of a coincidence as you think. Even in the larger African towns, tours like that are *the* cultural event of the year —of the decade. I tell you, I literally didn't see any real drama, any professional drama, for a decade after that tour. And when they come, everyone goes who has any pretensions to education. So if there's someone else here from any of the capitals they visited, it's perfectly natural that they saw her—almost inevitable."

"And you not only saw her . . ."

"That's right. It was my last few months at school. I'd organized a school party to the matinée, and helped get together a band of prefects from the school to act as ushers for all the performances. I was head boy, you see. I'm the sort who becomes head boy and never greatly distinguishes himself thereafter. I was invited to the party after the third and last performance, and . . . well, I was lucky. She was older than me— twenty-four, she said. Close to thirty, I imagine. She'd played Celia that night, and I thought she was enchanting. I realize now that she probably wasn't a very good actress. Certainly she never had much of a career. But I was . . . dazzled. And we went back to her hotel, and she was the first white woman I ever had. She was quite . . . remote. Now I realize why, but then I thought it was marvellous. She was so . . . ethereal. I know now that she was heterosexual only on occasion, maybe as a favour, almost. But to me that remoteness was stunning."

"And that was that, at the time?"

"Well, I suppose you could say so, though that sounds unromantic for how it actually felt. It was *the* great event of my adolescence, and it stayed with me. But, on a literal level, no, we did not keep in contact. Next day she was gone—to Lusaka, Kampala, or wherever. I never talked about it, still less about her, but her name was always with me: 'engraved on my heart,' as they used to say in the old-fashioned sort of romance."

"And it was the name you came across again?"

"Yes."

"Where?"

"Oddly enough, it was in *Twentieth-Century Romantic Novelists*. A big fat directory of all of us. You may have noticed that I'm very serious about studying trends, competition, markets. When I had my first romance accepted, I went to all the libraries in Nairobi trying to find out what I could about the romance game. I found this in the university library, and while I was stewing over it, her name—her real name—came out and hit me. It was like a revelation, an assertion of kinship! She hadn't gone on with her acting. She'd become a romantic novelist, like me!"

"You never doubted that she *had* written her books?"

"No. Why should I? She was in the book as Amanda Fairchild, pseudonym of Maureen Jane Shottery. I never had any suspicions, until I heard *after* her death. She never told me herself. It just tickled me, and I suppose appealed to my romantic side. I was pretty lonely for a time, after my . . . big love had died."

"You did nothing about it?"

"Not then, no. What could one do? I just read any of her books that came my way."

"You didn't recognize her in them?"

"No, but then, I wouldn't expect anyone to

recognize *me* in *mine*. And I really knew her so little."

"Fair enough. When eventually did you get in touch?"

"When I knew I was coming here. The fancy took me one night, when I was on my own. Her agent's name was in the directory where I'd found the name. I typed her a letter, reminded her very tactfully of the schoolboy she'd known in Nairobi in 1961, saying that by chance we'd both landed up in the same profession, and wondering whether she was coming to this conference."

"And she replied?"

"Eventually yes. I think she waited for a bit, wondering whether she should. But at last I got a letter, saying she would be here, that she'd be staying at the Kvalevåg guest-house, and hoping she'd see me. She said: 'Don't be put off by the performance I give—it's a relic of my old profession, and I regard it as part of my trade.' But she also said her acting days were so long in the past that she felt it was 'a quite different me' who had been Celia in *As You Like It*. She said: 'Let's meet as strangers and take it from there.'"

"And that's what you did. I never suspected any prior acquaintanceship, I must say."

"That was how she wanted it, and that was fine by me. But we did, of course, get together. We had the odd word, a few laughs, and she threw off the 'Amanda' bit the moment we were alone together, even for a moment . . . We sat together, remember, the first night in the bar. And on the second night she invited me along to her room. She had an empty room on one side, and the Finn on the other, so we could be discreet about it. I took along some of my books, we had a few drinks from her duty-free, and . . . we made love. Not very satisfactorily. I understood the problem now—and in fact she talked about it quite openly. But we were, we remained, very good friends."

"And in fact you went along a second time to her room on the night of the murder."

"To fetch my books! That much at least was true. And maybe to ask her if she'd like me to go along again later. I was just going out of la Zuckerman's sitting-room after my books when I remembered I'd left them with Maureen—Amanda. I went along there, but she wasn't in. The door was unlocked, though—somehow the usual precautions don't seem necessary in Norway—and I went in to look for them. They weren't in any of the obvious places—on the dressing-table, or the bedside table. Eventually I found them on the floor by, and half under, the bed. That's why I was so long away from the Zuckerman room."

"I see. And after the murder, you decided to lie."

"Yes. It was as simple as that. There was the sleeping with her, and the going along to her room at a time when she was out being murdered. I just hoped you wouldn't find out about the night we spent together."

"We did, in fact, have an attempt to pull the wool over our eyes about that."

"Oh? Who by?"

"Amanda's Australian editor."

"That rather drab-looking girl?"

"That's right. Robyn Harben. She tried to tell me that she, in fact, was Amanda's lover—implied she had been to bed with her out here."

"But you didn't believe her, though?"

"I half did at the time. But she was proved almost immediately after we'd finished talking to have told me one lie. She told me that she and Amanda became lovers soon after they first met, when Amanda was on an Australian tour. I learned immediately afterwards that Amanda had wangled a job for Robyn with Tamworth (Australia) even before that. Why would she do that? It was puzzling."

"And why should the girl say they were lesbian lovers if they weren't?"

"I think it was an extremely chivalrous attempt to keep hidden something she knew Amanda was ashamed of. Her lesbian tendencies she was not ashamed of—they were known, at least to a small circle. She didn't hide them from you, this time. So Robyn could claim that they were lovers without doing what she felt would be harm to her memory, harm to how she would like to be remembered. But the truth, I suspect—and I am only guessing here—is that Robyn was Amanda's *daughter*, and that she'd been given away at birth to an Australian couple."

"And it was that that Amanda was ashamed of?"

"That's my guess. It accounts for Amanda getting Robyn that job, even before they'd apparently met. It accounts for the *tone* of the letter she was writing just before she died, which was not that of lovers. Of course I think she was foolish to be ashamed: abortion was more difficult at that time, many people even then were crying out for babies to adopt, and an illegitimate baby would have been a hindrance in an acting career. Many women—and I suspect Amanda was one of them—are simply not maternal. How she got the baby adopted I can't say, but she may have been going out to Australia on another tour. Anyway, she felt guilty, and perhaps the fact that her career never really prospered afterwards confirmed her in her feelings of guilt. That's why she took on the Amanda impersonation—it was regular money. Anyway, Robyn was loyal to her feelings of shame at what she'd done. She kept the truth from me."

"How extraordinary."

"They did get on, I suspect, extremely well once they did meet up. That also came through in the note."

"It shows a remarkably fine nature."

"Yes, it does. And there's another thing about this girl that I think you ought to know."

"What's that?"

"She was born in 1962. The year after Amanda's African tour."

18

Untangled Skein

Half an hour later I was sitting with Stein and Svein in the little bedroom that they had taken over for their own use, reading the various reports that had come in about Amanda and some of the suspects. Some of these had come through my own contacts at Scotland Yard, but I was disappointed to see that they were no more revealing for that. One or two, however, did fill in the picture, as we were beginning to know it.

"There," I said, jabbing a finger at a report from someone who had once been (indeed, nominally still was at the time of her death) Amanda's agent for her stage work. "British Council tour of Central and Southern Africa in 1961. Then a J. C. Williamson tour of Australia in *The Constant Wife* in 1962–3. What's the betting she went out there early, had the baby, gave it to adoptive parents, and then went into rehearsal? . . . Now, what's this? Lorelei's record in the armed forces. Very sparse and formal."

"They don't give anything away," said Svein. "A lot of the time she was on confidential work."

"You mean spy stuff. I suppose that's where the story comes from that she worked for the CIA."

"That's right. What it was was interrogating suspected spies and potential defectors. There's a more informal report there somewhere from someone who worked with her at the same job —since retired, like her."

"Ah—here it is: 'adept at finding a weak place, then working and working at it till the suspect broke.' Well, that doesn't surprise me. Report from a man who was briefly her agent. Lorelei generally had to be kept away from fans and conventions of this sort because of her manner and tongue. Once told an interviewer on a Midwest television station that she'd taken up with the hearts and flowers market because it was the one literary form where you could have a complete contempt for your audience. Wow! That must have set the telephone lines buzzing! What else? . . . Police reports . . . Patti Drewe suspected of fiddling welfare payments for her sick husband twelve years ago. Hmmm. Nothing there, surely? Anyway, welfare in the States is so tiny it wouldn't keep a dog alive. More power to her elbow . . . Maryloo Parker arrested in 1969 on suspicion of soliciting. Released for lack of evidence. Quite right: that's her natural manner."

"Not much there," said Stein, in his soft little voice. "Or not much to the purpose."

"Not much at all," I agreed. "Nothing to establish anything like a motive. Dislike isn't a motive. Rivalry isn't a motive. Having slept with someone who didn't greatly enjoy it isn't a motive. There's nothing that we really want here."

I got up and walked to the window. Down below in the garden Cristobel and Bernard were walking. Theirs had to be the most peripatetic romance since the Pardoner and the Summoner. They were holding hands and swinging their arms backwards and forwards. Really! Cristobel was a lumpish thirty-odd, and Bernard a bony about-the-same. A spasm of irritation shot through me. The trouble with my family was that they never grew up. The trouble with me, Jan sometimes says, is that I grew up too soon.

Stein was speaking, even more slowly than usual. He had been thinking about my last remarks.

"You say they throw no light on *motive*. Does that mean you think you know how it was done?"

I turned back from the window and looked at him.

"I *think* so."

"And who did it?"

"That too. At least, I'd take a bet on it. No certainty. And any 'evidence' I have is not lawcourt evidence at all."

"No conviction?"

"No conviction—sorry. Unless your boys can dig up something substantial, something that will hold."

"Are you going to tell me?"

I smiled.

"Are you going to let me go? I have a few days of holiday left, and I'd very much rather spend them in the mountains with my wife and son than here."

Stein spread his hands.

"We can't keep you indefinitely. We can't keep any of these people much longer. Tell us what you think, and you're free to go when you like. As far as I can see, practically any of them could have done it."

"That's right. *Practically* any of them. The woman I saw come through the lounge and go out to the boathouse *was* Amanda—I saw her face, from three or four yards' distance. Normally Amanda might be quite easy to impersonate—floppy hat, big, obvious coats. But there is no question of that: I saw her face, and she had no accessories, she was quite simply dressed. It *was* Amanda. That being so, I myself would rule out Patti Drewe, Mrs. Biggs and Lorelei Zuckerman, because their activities are vouched for pretty reliably all through the relevant time. Any of the rest could have done it."

"Some being more likely than others?" Stein hazarded.

"Maybe," I said. "Basically their eligibility as suspects consists in each case of trips away from the scene—to the loo, to bedrooms, to get drinks—trips which in fact may have been longer than they needed to be, and in one case must have been longer than it needed to be. Of course, in the nature of things, and with a lot of drinking going on, or even just a certain amount of it, other people failed to notice. To me, then, all the rest are possibles. For example, the idea that Arthur Biggs was at the loo for only two minutes depends on the evidence of his wife. And when you look at their relationship—which is based on the desire to be worshipped and the willingness to worship—then the evidence is next to totally useless."

I looked back into the garden. Bernard and Cristobel were sitting on the far seat, on the other side of the lawn, holding hands. Cristobel was gazing into Bernard's eyes in the generally approved manner, and he was apparently finding this acceptable. Some relationships are based on funny things, I thought.

"What is this evidence that is not evidence that leads you to prefer one of them over the rest, then?" asked Svein.

"First, an empty bottle," I said, turning back. "A nice produceable piece of evidence, you might think. But the *smell* is not produceable. I kick myself that I didn't think about it at the time. I was rooting round behind the boathouse before you came, with Amanda's body still lying there. And there was this empty bottle in the undergrowth, and this strong smell of alcohol."

"We found the bottle next day," said Stein. "We still have it, of course. What's so significant about it?"

"An empty bottle, thrown away, doesn't smell strongly of alcohol. Only if the bottle had alcohol in it when it was thrown away would you get the sort of smell I noticed. Now who in Norway throws away bottles with alcohol in it?"

"Nobody," said Svein, the expert, promptly.

"The only thing that might happen is somebody dropping and spilling a bottle with some in when they are dead drunk."

"Quite. And does it often happen?"

"Hardly ever. Because they cling on to it like death."

"Exactly. I can't see even Martti letting his grip slacken on a bottle that had something in it. You cling on to it like death because it's so bloody expensive here."

"So?"

"And when you're away at a conference or something, and you're having drinks together— as Wes Mackay had drinks with Amanda—what do you do? If you're foreign, you get together and you drink your duty-free."

"Of course," agreed Svein. "It happens all the time in Norwegian hotels. That's why the bars are so empty."

"And yet when Lorelei invited Mackay and Leino up to her room, little Miss Maxwell went down to the bar three times in order to fetch drinks."

"But," objected Stein, after he'd thought about it, "Mrs. Zuckerman drinks a lot of brandy and water, doesn't she? She'd probably drunk her duty-free."

"In three days? And these are inter-continental travellers: they have double the allowance of European travellers. And yet, ignoring all the duty-free in the room, everyone has what they want, and Felicity goes and gets it from the bar. If Lorelei went on drinking her own brandy, as she says she did, then that is two rounds for three, at over a hundred kroner per round. Two rounds at over ten pounds or fifteen dollars each —and then one round just for Martti at thirty-odd kroner."

"It's a lot of money," admitted Stein.

"And though it was Amanda who was the obviously tight-fisted one, does la Zuckerman strike you as the type who would joyously shell out for bar drinks for an alcoholic Finn who could never get enough?"

"No," said Stein.

"Could it be, in fact, that Martti was asked because he was an alcoholic, and could be relied upon to have a hazy memory, and because he drank vodka, which Felicity Maxwell had a supply of in her room?"

"Only of course it was the wrong kind," said Svein, who had a sharp brain and an excellent memory.

"Exactly. Not something she could have foreseen. Martti drank only, or for preference, Smirnoff, which is what they stock in the bar. The bar is very tiny: it only has one brand of each drink. Yet Martti's third drink, when she got one for him alone, was the wrong brand. She relied on Wes Mackay not noticing how long she was gone, because she wasn't getting drinks for him. What she couldn't foresee was that the *brand* would be noticed by Martti. The frustrating thing is, Martti's the sort who would know, and yet there's not a juryman in the world who would put any weight on his word."

Stein nodded sadly in agreement.

"This is how I see the whole set-up. Some time

earlier in the day Felicity broaches the matter of a meeting with Amanda, and mentions the boat-house. There is a developing hostility between Amanda and la Zuckerman, though Felicity is not to know that Amanda does not take it too seriously—merely enjoys it with the actress part of her nature. No doubt Felicity needed to say little more than that she had information about Lorelei that Amanda might find interesting, and that she'd get a note with the time on it to her some way or other—put it in her hand, slip it under her door, or whatever. Lorelei is a demanding mistress, she might say, with truth, and she doesn't know when she can get away. When they've set up the meeting with the boys in Lorelei's room, she decides on that night. And while she is fetching the first or second round of drinks, she slips into the little room off the lounge and types the note, setting 9:30 as the time for the meeting. She will guess that by about then Martti will be in need of another drink, but she and Wes are drinking much more slowly, Wes particularly taking care, since his hostess is paying, not something likely to bother Martti. OK so far?"

"Sure," said the Norwegian.

"So Felicity that evening fetches a first round of drinks from the bar, then fetches a second. Probably with the second she fetches a lot of ice —more than she needs. As she could obviously expect, by 9:20 Martti's glass is empty. She takes it into her room, fills it with ice and vodka from her duty-free supply, then takes the bottle with her when she goes down the back stairs, through the kitchen, and out the least obtrusive way to the boathouse."

"Why does she take the bottle?"

"Because as soon as we see that she has vodka in her room, we might ask why she hadn't supplied Martti's needs with that. Right, now: on the way down on that back path towards the boathouse, which only has a few feet across the lawn before taking the normal path down to the water, she collects a cherry blossom bough from the tree under Amanda's window, to give the corpse a romantic hallmark. When she gets there Amanda is waiting, she starts talking, then fells Amanda with a blow, holds her head under the water, then throws the cherry blossom bough on top of the corpse. Before going back to the house, she tips away the vodka behind the boathouse, and discards the bottle. Then it's back to her bedroom to collect Martti's vodka, and back into Lorelei's sitting-room."

The other two sat thinking for a minute or two.

"There's two things I don't understand," said Svein, "and one is why do it at all? Somehow we've got to find that out. But the other is, why the cherry blossom? Why tie it down to the romantic conference, to Amanda's last book? Why not kick her out into the fjord? Surely any normal murderer would at least attempt to make it look like an ordinary drowning?"

"Yes, those are questions," I said, getting up. "To be precise, they are questions for you. I've given you my ideas, and now I think I may be allowed to go and join my family." I put my voice into falsetto and sang "The hills are alive with the sound of music." I realized it is not as easy to imitate Julie Andrews as Julie Andrews makes it sound. My performance was greeted with silence. I looked down at the garden, where Cristobel and Bernard had resumed their swinging-arms routine, interspersing it with their locking-eyes routine in a thoroughly nauseating manner.

Stein and Svein had come to join me by the window. Stein said: "There's more, isn't there?"

I nodded.

"If you don't mind the most blatant conjecture. Though perhaps it's a bit more than that. Perhaps we could call it the logical progression from what I've just said. Say we grant that Felicity Maxwell did the murder. We then ask ourselves the question: why did Lorelei Zuckerman ask Wes and Martti to her room that night."

"You think it was uncharacteristic?"

"I know it was uncharacteristic. We all commented on it at the time. And if we grant that Lorelei, by some quirk of fancy, did such an unlikely thing, why didn't she have Felicity offer them drink from her own duty-free stocks? The answer is: Lorelei was part of the set-up."

"Used by Felicity?" asked Svein incredulously.

"No, using Felicity. A commissioned murder. And one which brazenly announces itself as a murder. Let's take the question of the cherry blossom bough. Why throw it on the body at all?"

"I thought it must be to mislead," said Svein.

"Exactly. That's the first possibility. To suggest that the murder had something to do with the romantic writers, when in fact it was nothing to do with them at all. But whom do we have on the suspect list who is *not* connected with the Romantic Novelists' Conference?"

"The Bavarians, and the American family?" suggested Stein.

"Precisely. And have you managed to nose out any connection between them and Amanda?" Stein shook his head. "Now what other possible reason could there be for the cherry blossom bough?"

The other two shook their heads slowly, but Svein said: "It seemed almost like—a piece of theatre."

"Yes," I said. "Something of that kind. A theatrical touch, a challenge. Who might gild the lily in that way?"

"A madman?" suggested Svein. "Someone puffed up with his own conceit—maybe Arthur Biggs, perhaps?"

"Yes. But he is not the only one who is sick with self-love. Lorelei is another, and I believe she organized the murder for pleasure, having nothing to lose. Murder is the ultimate assertion of power over another person. Asserting power, in different ways, is something Lorelei has been doing all her life. And Lorelei gives this last assertion a further twist: she asserts power over the victim, and over the murderer."

"But I still don't see: *why* the cherry blossom?" asked Stein.

"Have you noticed what pleasure she gets out

of tyrannizing over a cool, independent girl like Miss Maxwell? A cruder lover of power might tyrannize over a drudge, but Lorelei is an epicure. Similarly with murder: someone else might hug themselves over murdering a total stranger—knowing he will get away with it because there is nothing to connect him with his victim. To that extent Agatha Christie was right: murder is easy. But what satisfaction can be got out of something that is *easy*, that anyone could do? Lorelei has a horrendous sense of her own greatness. *Her* murder must announce itself. She must challenge the police to pin it on her."

"Hence the rivalry with Amanda," said Svein.

"Exactly. She engineers the rivalry, by a most unusual degree of accommodatingness (not friendliness, or niceness—she could never have managed that). Thus she is murdering someone she is known to be competing with to be the centrepiece of the conference. Amanda was chosen as the victim because Lorelei was the *most* likely murderer in every way except physically. The cherry blossom was a challenge. I can murder, I can be the most likely murderer, I can announce the motive, yet I can get away with it. And she's right. She will."

"But why would the girl go along with that?"

"Ah—that you would have to find out. And, having found out, see if you can break her. But I don't think you will find it as easy to break her as would appear. She is no fragile little blossom herself. There's a vein of iron somewhere there. Just the manner of the murder tells you that."

Stein looked me in the eye.

"You have a suggestion as to where I should start looking, haven't you?"

"I would have thought the mother's death, wouldn't you? Just look at the facts: the mother dies, and Felicity goes straight from nursing her to nursing Lorelei next door. It's not natural, whatever the girl herself may say. Did Lorelei know something, and hold it over Felicity? And if I were you, I'd try to find out whether the girl took judo classes, or something of that sort. It's a natural thing for a young girl living alone or with another, older woman to take, living in New York. She'd need something like that to kill Amanda quickly and easily—so quickly and easily that she cannot have got herself wet, or no wetter than could dry off in a few minutes. It was a very dexterous kill, and she had to have the training. The investigation in detail is up to you. Keep me informed . . ."

I looked down again at the lawn, and the couple who were now sitting cross-legged and giggling together.

"Do you have a father?" asked Stein.

"No, my father—died."

"I think you'll soon be giving your sister away."

I sighed.

"I rather think I will."

And, really, I may as well jump ahead a bit in time and announce it in the approved manner.

Reader, she married him.

19

Epilogue

I kept in touch with Stein Bjørhovde from Oppheim, where we walked through flower-strewn meadows and ate the most predictable food. Jan was annoyed that I had picked on anyone other than Arthur Biggs as the murderer, but Stein and Svein were brought round entirely to my way of thinking by their interrogations of the two people involved. What they could not do, though, was pin the murder on them, and in the end, in one of our last telephone conversations, I was reduced to pointing out that the real perpetrator was Lorelei Zuckerman, and that she had received a death sentence anyway.

I was most interested in the subject of Felicity Maxwell's mother, and the circumstances of her death. It seemed a remote chance, but I wondered if, when the matter was brought up again, the New York police would find any way of pinning that killing on to her. It was, after all, a killing much closer to her, with a more easily definable motive.

I heard the details of this a week after I'd left Kvalevåg, on my first day back at the Yard. Joplin had got the details for me, and I studied them with interest. Homicide in New York had indeed been less than happy about this death, but there was evidence that Mrs. Maxwell, though not an old woman, was an alcoholic and depressive, as well as being an incurable invalid, and had had the habit of pretending to suffocate herself on the grounds that her daughter didn't love her and wanted her dead. They came to the conclusion that in one of these performances fluid had collected in the bronchial tube to such a degree that she died even though she had thrown the bedding off her face. They were helped to this conclusion by the testimony of a neighbour who dropped into the apartment and was talking to the daughter of the dead woman almost at the moment of death—indeed, while they were talking they heard choking sounds from the bedroom. By the time they got there the woman was dead. The neighbour, of course, was a Mrs. Zuckerman.

The New York police could see little to be gained by reopening the case, and I could see their point. They had doubtless had three or four thousand murders in the city since the death of Mrs. Maxwell, and there was little enough reason to revive that particular inquiry rather than any other of the unsolved thousands. One could only take the view that the deed had indeed been manslaughter, and that the perpetrator had been sufficiently punished by being pressed into the service of Lorelei Zuckerman for her dying years. Still, one would dearly like to have known what exactly Lorelei overheard in that flat.

And I would have liked, still more, to have confirmation of the reason why Mrs. Zuckerman had had her companion kill Amanda Fairchild.

Stein and Svein had kept Lorelei and Felicity longer than the others at Kvalevåg, but eventually they had had to let them go. I rang them to tell them my information about Felicity's mother, which they in fact already had a version of. I asked when the two women were travelling home, and was told next day: they were flying SAS to Heathrow, then PanAm from Heathrow to New York. I found this interesting. I thought it might be only when they were out of London, practically on home territory, that they would do any talking about the subject that must be closest to them—if, indeed, they did any talking at all.

I got on to the travel people at the Yard, to find out if there were any of our people due to travel to New York in the near future. I found that there were two due to go by BA the next day, to take part in an on-the-streets investigation into an international drug ring. One was Melvin Porter, of the Drugs Squad, the other was a relatively new policeman called Dexter, or Charlie Peace. I knew Charlie well, from the time when he had helped me enormously in the investigation into the minor massacre at the *Bodies* office. He was new in the Force to be

chosen for an international assignment, and the
fact that he was black had obviously helped.
Why it had obviously helped an investigation
into the New York drug scene I had better not
say, lest this book be accused of negative stereo-
typing, or some such crime.

Their booking was changed, and I arranged
with PanAm that they were to be placed beside
and behind Zuckerman and Maxwell, and arranged with Charlie and Melvin Porter how
they were to act, how be dressed. I rather
thought that Charlie, being black, would be
treated by la Zuckerman as lower than dirt,
hardly worth consideration as part of the human
race. This is what I was counting on, and this was
how it turned out. I heard from Charlie briefly
by phone when he arrived in New York, more
fully by letter a few days later. I give you the
relevant part of what he wrote.

I didn't enjoy this dame's choice of airline, for
a start. To have to *pay* to watch the in-flight
movie! I didn't want to watch it, and I had my
assignment from you anyway, but it's the
principle that counts, and the principle is
lousy. Mel tells me all airline food tastes the
same, so I'll say nothing about that. Anyway, I
got to my seat early, in my young executive
suit, clutching my initialled briefcase on my
lap—they weren't my initials, but it all added
to the picture.

They came on the plane almost last. They
could have got on first, she being an invalid,
but I guess she likes to make an entrance. It

was very hot, and she was wearing this shiny black dress, and she was helped along the gangway from behind by Miss Maxwell, having ignored the stewardess's offers of help. I was on the gangway, and they had the seats nearest the window. I got up to let her through. She'd shot me a look when she saw she was sitting next to a black, then she ignored the politeness. Miss Maxwell took the window seat, because Zuckerman said there was nothing to see anyway. As she got herself into her seat, she said:

"When I joined up in the army, they only greased the trucks and carried the garbage. By the time I got out they'd practically taken over . . . Now they wear suits and carry briefcases."

So that put me pleasantly in my place.

I sat myself down again, put my briefcase under my legs, and pretended I wasn't there. It's an ingrained racial gift, you know. I loved my first take-off, and endured the first serving of food. Zuckerman and Maxwell ate, in silence. Zuckerman demanded a brandy, then another. It didn't seem like nerves, though, just habit. After they'd taken away the trays I settled down to pretended sleep. Though I needn't have bothered, because the Zuckerman never looked my way or gave the slightest sign that she was aware of my presence. The seat next to her might have been empty. I was a non-person.

It was when we had been in the air a couple of hours—boy, this flight was more gruelling than I had expected!—that the Maxwell girl spoke, quite low.

"Well, that went off all right."

Long silence. The Maxwell girl seemed used to that, and she just sat there. Zuckerman was smoking a cigarillo. Eventually she spoke.

"Of course. I knew it would."

The Maxwell girl sipped at her drink, and looked out on to the cloud.

"I feel I've worked out my sentence."

Zuckerman like a flash leaned across and hissed:

"Remember, you can have no hold over a dying woman."

A long time later, when most people around were watching the film, and I was apparently in deep sleep, the Maxwell girl said:

"You know, I never understood *why*."

There was a long pause, then Zuckerman said, quite distinctly:

"Because it was something I'd never done . . . And you had. Murder is *the* ultimate thing to have done, don't you find?"

Felicity Maxwell said sadly: "No. I don't find that."

They were mostly silent for the rest of the flight.

About the Author

ROBERT BARNARD, a four-time Edgar nominee, is one of the top names in mystery writing today. His most recent books are *Bodies*, *Political Suicide*, *Fête Fatale*, and *Out of the Blackout*. He lives in Leeds, England.